D1575184

TEEN SCIENCE FICTION DR. WHO
McCormack, Una.
 The way through the woods

DOCTOR ⟨⟩ WHO

The Way through the Woods

The DOCTOR WHO series from BBC Books

Available now:

Apollo 23 *by Justin Richards*

Night of the Humans *by David Llewellyn*

The Forgotten Army *by Brian Minchin*

Nuclear Time *by Oli Smith*

The King's Dragon *by Una McCormack*

The Glamour Chase *by Gary Russell*

Dead of Winter *by James Goss*

The Way through the Woods *by Una McCormack*

Hunter's Moon *by Paul Finch*

Coming soon:

Touched by an Angel *by Jonathan Morris*

Paradox Lost *by George Mann*

Borrowed Time *by Naomi Alderman*

DOCTOR WHO

The Way through the Woods

UNA McCORMACK

3 5 7 9 10 8 6 4

Published in 2011 by BBC Books, an imprint of Ebury Publishing
A Random House Group Company

Copyright © Una McCormack 2011

Una McCormack has asserted her right to be identified as author of this
Work in accordance with the Copyright, Designs and Patents Act 1988.

Doctor Who is a BBC Wales production for BBC One.
Executive producers: Steven Moffat, Piers Wenger and Beth Willis

BBC, DOCTOR WHO and TARDIS (word marks, logos and devices) are
trademarks of the British Broadcasting Corporation and are used under
licence.

The Random House Group Limited Reg. No. 954009

Addresses for companies within the Random House Group can be found
at www.randomhouse.co.uk

A catalogue record for this book is available from the British Library

ISBN 978 1 849 90237 3

The Random House Group Limited supports The Forest Stewardship
Council (FSC®), the leading international forest certification organisation.
Our books carrying the FSC label are printed on FSC® certified paper.
FSC is the only forest certification scheme endorsed by the leading environmental
organisations, including Greenpeace. Our paper procurement policy can be found at
www.randomhouse.co.uk/environment

Commissioning editor: Albert DePetrillo
Editorial manager: Nicholas Payne
Series consultant: Justin Richards
Project editor: Steve Tribe
Cover design: Lee Binding © Woodlands Books Ltd 2011
Production: Rebecca Jones

Printed and bound in Great Britain by Clays Ltd, St Ives plc

To buy books by your favourite authors and register for offers,
visit www.randomhouse.co.uk

For Kat,
who also likes Amy

Between the housing estate and the motorway lies an ancient wood. Birds live there, and foxes, and the many small beasts that snuffle round the undergrowth busy on their own quiet errands. The woods teem with life: sharp, clever robins and blackbirds with bright and restless eyes; owls that sleep by day and quest by night; vivid darting butterflies; and all the wild and thrilling creatures – badgers, and hares, and maybe even a glimpse of a soft-eyed, soft-footed deer with her small fawn. Yes, the woods are filled with life.

But not with people. People – human people – don't go near the woods. The birds are left to nest in peace, the foxes to trot and hunt, the many small beasts to run and hide. And if, on a clear bright day, you took to the skies and you flew high, high above the land, you would see the trees gathered thickly in their hollow, old and dark and patient. You would see how the housing estate backs away from the forest, and you would see too how the motorway strains and bends to avoid it. Screwing up your eyes, you would look for a path leading into the woods – but you would not find one. Because there is no way through the woods. There has never been a way through the woods.

Chapter
1

England, autumn, just before the ten o'clock news

Vicky Caine's watch was a sixteenth birthday present from her dad. Vicky Caine's dad was short of cash that month, and the watch was of doubtful origin. But Vicky didn't mind. She appreciated the thought, and she'd almost saved up enough from babysitting to get a proper watch, if she really wanted one. Besides, after sixteen years, Vicky had a pretty good idea of what her dad was like. Fun, but not what you would call reliable.

Unfortunately for Vicky, her dad's gift wasn't very reliable either. Vicky Caine's watch had stopped twenty-two minutes earlier, but Vicky didn't know that yet.

She was babysitting that evening for her parents' friends Carole and Frank, who were at their dancing class. (Carole had made Frank take up tango because of Vincent on *Strictly Come Dancing*.) Vicky took their little boy Alfie up to bed at seven o'clock, read him his Charlie and Lola book (twice), and then she settled down in front of the television. Vicky liked BBC Four, but her older brother, Mark, laughed at her whenever she switched it on at home. Now she had four straight hours, curled up in Carole's brown leather sofa, undisturbed by brothers or fathers. Bliss. Partway through a documentary about the Ancient Greeks, Carole and Frank came back in, cheerful from the exercise. They all had a cup of tea and a chat, and then Vicky noticed the time on her watch. Five to ten.

'Hey,' she said, 'I'm going to miss my bus! I'd better run!'

She grabbed her coat, and gave Carole a quick kiss, waving away Frank's offer of a lift, as she did every week. No point in that when the bus took Vicky almost to her front door. Frank watched her to the end of the street. The stop was no more than minute's walk from there.

It was a chilly night, late in October. During the day there was still bright sunlight and blue skies, but by this time there was a sharp edge to the air, as if the evening had suddenly drawn in its breath. Vicky stood beneath the dull orange street lamp, stamped her feet, and hummed contentedly to herself. After a few minutes, she started to get impatient. 'Come on bus,' she shivered. The last bus was often a bit late. Especially when it was cold.

Another few minutes, and she started to feel uneasy. She pushed up her glove to check the time.

Five to ten.

'Oh, you're *kidding* me...' Vicky tapped the face of the watch. The hands remained locked in place, frozen at an earlier time. 'Oh, *Dad*...'

Who knew what time it was now? Had the bus come or gone? After a couple more minutes of indecision, Vicky heard, very faintly, blown towards her on the slight breeze, the town hall clock. It was chiming the quarter-hour.

That cleared it up, then. She'd missed her bus by a good ten minutes. So what now? She debated popping back and taking up that offer of a lift, but knocking at the door would almost certainly wake up Alfie, and she really didn't want to drag Frank out. Taxi? Vicky sighed as she took out her phone. Taxis were *so* expensive.

No signal. She really was short of luck

tonight. There was nothing else for it…

'Mum'll kill me if she ever finds out,' Vicky murmured, as she set off down the lane. Still, now she had a twenty-minute walk to think up a good cover story. What time did that Ancient Greek thing end? She could say she stayed to watch it to the finish, and then suggest that she'd got a lift… Not outright lie, just *hint*… OK, so Mark would never shut up about it, but even that was better than admitting she'd walked home…

A walk which, so it turned out, was going to take longer than Vicky expected. Barely had she left the bus stop, when the lane started bending in the wrong direction, back towards the houses and away from the junction with Mill Road, where Vicky lived. She tried to picture the route the lane took, but couldn't fix on anything substantial. She had a hazy sense that at some point it had to meet up with Mill Road. Why would a road wander like this? Weren't roads meant to be straight, if at all possible?

'Must be a contour line,' Vicky mumbled to no one in particular. On the bus she had never noticed; she must always have been reading or listening to music. But it was going to add absolutely *ages* to her walk. 'I am in *so* much trouble,' Vicky told the cold clear sky. Some stars twinkled back, sympathetically, but didn't deign to offer any advice. She tried her phone every so often, but still couldn't get a signal. Must be some kind of dead spot, around the edge of the estate.

At last, the houses came to an end. Ahead, the lane curved on, lit at intervals by orange lamps that still bent gently away from where Vicky wanted to be. She stopped to get the lie of the land. In the distance, far behind and to her left, she could hear the soft throb of traffic on the motorway; the sound of safety, of civilisation. The new estate was behind her too, over on the right. Looking back over her shoulder at it, Vicky saw bright squares of light in upstairs windows where the curtains had not yet been drawn: people going to bed on an ordinary Tuesday night, everyday signs of everyday life. Carole and Frank would probably be in bed now, their house in darkness. No, Vicky didn't want to disturb them.

The town hall clock chimed half past ten. Vicky looked ahead. On either side of her lay open ground, fields, cloaked in darkness, although looking straight across the left-hand side she could see what she thought were the street lights at the junction where the lane eventually met Mill Road. Why couldn't a lane simply go *straight* when you most needed it? She crossed the road and stopped at the fence, looking at the beacon of light at the junction. If she cut across the field, she would get straight there. But cutting across the field would bring her very close…

To Swallow Woods.

Vicky shivered again. The woods were creepy. Everyone knew and everyone kept away. Parents didn't have to issue warnings because kids didn't even dare each other to go near. Vicky had never heard a reason, not a particular reason, but everyone knew to keep their distance from Swallow Woods. Probably it was nothing more than children's tales; a memory of a dark and wild place glimpsed when you were small that somehow stuck with you, even when you were old enough to know better.

But the truth was that, right now, Vicky was far more worried about what her mum was going to say when she rolled up well after eleven o'clock. A kid's tale about a scary forest was nowhere near as scary as Vicky's mum when she thought one of her children had done something particularly irresponsible. Vicky rested her hand on the rough wooden fence and stared at the lights twinkling and beckoning over at the junction. If you thought about it, the woods were pretty much the safest place in the area – nobody went anywhere near them. This was the twenty-first century, not the dark ages, and Vicky was sixteen, not six. Who believed there were monsters in the woods?

The decision made, Vicky climbed over the fence and jumped down. She landed with a soft thud on compacted earth, and she was heartened to realise that this was a footpath of sorts. So other people did come this way and, looking at the path, it seemed they did so for the same reason as her: to cut off the loop in the lane and to get as quickly as possible to the junction with the road. So there was no reason to go near the trees. She could steer by the lights, and follow the path. There was no need to go anywhere near the trees. Not that it would matter. It wouldn't matter at all.

The trees sat patiently, a dark and silent mass to her left. Vicky kept her eyes firmly fixed on the street lights. The path quickly became muddier, a mess of tufts of thick grass and clods of wet earth. The ground sloped down to the left, and it proved difficult for Vicky not to be drawn that way. As if the trees were acting like a magnet... but trees couldn't do that, of course.

'You're spooking yourself,' Vicky said. 'You're being stupid.' Her voice came out high and rather thin, but firm enough to be a comfort. She shoved her hands deep into her coat pockets and plodded on.

Then she slipped – on a lump of soil, perhaps, or a tough piece of grass. She fell forwards, tumbling down onto the ground, rolling heavily onto one side. She sat still for a few moments, eyes closed, arms wrapped around her body, making herself take deep breaths until the sick shaky feeling passed and she was sure she wasn't going to burst into tears. She longed to be home, taking her ear-bashing from Mum, bickering with Mark.

Vicky opened her eyes. There was mud all over her coat, her jeans, and her boots. 'I'm in so much trouble...' She stood up, brushing uselessly at herself, only succeeding in smearing mud over more of her clothes. 'Wait till it dries,' she told herself. 'Clean it in the morning. When you're home.' She looked round. Clouds had covered the sky and the stars had slipped quietly away. She could no longer see street lights, in any direction.

For one brief, awful second, Vicky panicked. She heard herself moan, and she clamped her hand over her mouth. 'You have to go *up*,' she whispered into her glove. 'The trees are in the hollow. If you go *up*, you'll find the road.' And as soon as she found the road, she would stick to it. She would never come this way again. She would never come this near to the trees. It wasn't worth it.

She took one tentative step forwards. Then another, then another. She wasn't certain, but it felt like she was going up. But the night was very dark now, and the throb of the motorway very distant, and a hill can rise again before sloping away. The trees were silent and invisible, and long before she realised what she had done, Vicky entered their embrace. A fox, which had been sitting and watching with interest as she stumbled ever nearer to the woods, sniffed at the chill night air, coughed, and then trotted after her. And that was the last anyone saw of Vicky Caine for quite some time.

Chapter
2

England, autumn 1917, shortly before closing time

Emily Bostock smiled at the young man sitting by himself at the far side of the pub. He smiled back, as he had done every time. Nice smile, this one, perhaps a bit lop-sided and not so sure of itself, but kind, Emily thought. Yes, he looked very kind.

Annie, the landlady, tapped Emily on the arm. 'There's a table over there that could do with a wipe.' She nodded towards the young man and gave Emily a conspiratorial wink. 'That table too, maybe, on your way back?'

'Maybe,' Emily said, not wanting to commit herself. No need to rush now, was there? Where did that get you?

'He looks nice,' Annie said. 'That's all I'm saying.'

Emily picked up a cloth and gave it a shake. 'Never said he didn't, did I?'

Annie laughed. Emily, smiling, headed off to gather up empty glasses, swapping a few words with the regulars as she went round. She kept half an eye on the nice young man, though, wondering who he was, where he'd come from. She'd never seen him before this evening. He had walked in twenty minutes after they reopened, eaten a huge piece of pie, and sat there in his corner ever since, sipping at one pint of ale. He stuck out like old Frank's red nose, and he'd earned himself a fair amount of muttered comment from Frank and his cronies as a result. Not just because he was a stranger, but because he was young. Only the old men drank at the Fox these days. The young men were all gone away.

'Well,' Emily said briskly, clattering the glasses together, 'there it is.' She glanced again at the young man. Good gracious, he was staring right at her! That was forward! Emily blushed hotly. Frank and his gang of old wasps hadn't missed it either; the story would be round the village in no time. Emily hurried her pile of glasses into the back, where she lingered over the washing up and wondered whatever this young stranger could be about.

When she came out front again, an unpleasant silence was hanging around the bar, like dirty old smog over a city. The young man was still sitting by himself, but now he was staring down at a white feather that had somehow found its way onto the table in front of him. He seemed bewildered, like he couldn't quite believe what he was looking at.

Emily saw red. Hadn't this lot done enough damage by now? Weren't they satisfied? Annie gave her a worried glance and opened her mouth to speak, but before she could get a word out, Emily called across to the young man, making sure her voice carried to every nook and cranny of the pub. 'Don't you pay any attention to this lot,' she said. 'The closest any one of them's been to France is a day trip to Brighton.'

The silence in the room changed, like everyone had stopped hungering for a reaction and instead suddenly became embarrassed or ashamed. So they should be. Blood pumping in her ears, Emily threw her dish cloth over her shoulder and stalked back out. Slowly, she washed her face and hands in the big sink, cooling her cheeks and her head. Funny how she didn't want to cry. This time last year she would have been in floods. Perhaps she was past that now. She wasn't sure whether that was a good or a bad sign. She didn't ever want to forget...

When Emily came out front again, hardly any of the drinkers met her eye, and those who did quickly looked away. So they should. The evening was quiet after that, subdued, and when Annie rang the bell for closing time, Emily made a big show of walking over to the young man. 'If you wait,' she said, loud enough for everyone to hear, 'you can walk me home.'

She heard the stir behind her. She tossed her head.

The young man glanced past her, rather nervously. But he said, 'Great! Yeah! I'll wait. Of course I'll wait!'

Annie didn't make her stay. 'I'll clear up. Don't want to keep him hanging around while you wash up, do you?'

So Emily washed her hands again, straightened her hair, and pinned on her hat, the one with the jet-black butterfly pinned to the crown. It wasn't her best hat, but it was definitely an eye-catcher. A proven success. The young man stood by the door and smiled at her as he waited.

'What's your name, then?' she said.

'Rory.' He was twiddling with the white feather between his fingers. They were long, expressive fingers that looked like they might do much of his talking for him.

'Just Rory? Nothing else? Or do you come with a whole name of your very own?'

He laughed. 'Williams. Rory Williams.'

She stuck out her hand, feeling very modern. 'And I'm Emily Bostock. Very pleased to make your acquaintance, Mr Williams.'

He shook her hand. 'The pleasure's all mine, Miss Bostock.' Then, sweetly, he took her shawl and placed it around her shoulders. Nice smile, and nice manners too.

'Well,' Emily said. 'Are you going to walk me home or not?'

'I think I should.' He pushed the door open, stood back, and bowed. 'After you, Miss Bostock.'

'Why, thank you, Mr Williams!'

Outside a nearly full moon poured milky light upon the lane. The sky itself was stained indigo dark and there was a faint bite to the air. Emily pulled her shawl tighter around herself and glanced back at her companion. His face was in shadow as he closed the door behind them. Now they were alone together. All of a sudden, Emily felt shy. Not such the modern girl after all, was she? And it was a while since she'd been by herself with a young man.

They stood on the step staring at each other, warm yellow lamplight spilling onto them through the windows of the pub. Yes, he had a nice face this one, not what you'd call striking, not exactly, and with a few worry lines, but, well – *nice*. Suddenly Emily felt quite breathless, like she was doing something she oughtn't, but didn't care. She felt quite free.

'Er,' her companion said, after a moment or two standing like this. He lifted his finger as if wanting to attract her attention, while not actually causing any bother, 'I don't know, you know, where you live…'

'Oh, of course, silly me!' Emily pointed past the grey silhouette of the old mill towards Long Lane, winding its way across the darkened fields. 'Out that way. Not quite four miles.' She bit her lip. 'Not too far for you, is it?'

'No, not at all.' He offered her his arm; she linked her own through it, and they walked companionably down the road and turned onto Long Lane. Williams had turned shy; he would catch her eye, open his mouth to start up a conversation and then close his mouth again and smile at her instead. With his free hand, he was still fiddling with the white feather. Maybe that was what was making him bashful.

'I hope you're not too upset about that,' Emily said, nodding towards the feather. 'Nobody with any sense hands them out. Disgusting thing to do, if you ask me.'

'Sorry, what?'

'Your white feather. You weren't too upset by all that business, were you?'

He looked at the feather, as if he hardly remembered he still had it. He gave a nervous laugh. 'Upset? Why would I be upset?'

'Well, you know…' Emily tried to think of a delicate way of putting it, because you couldn't outright say to a young man, particularly such a nice young man, *They think you're a coward because you're not in uniform.* 'They give them to those who haven't been out there… You know. As an insult.'

The penny dropped. 'Oh! Yeah, I see. Probably should have thought of that.'

'Maybe next time keep your silver badge on or something. Well, I'm glad you weren't offended, Mr Williams, but where've you been that you don't know what handing out a white feather means?'

'Here and there.' He waved the feather around vaguely. 'You know how it is.'

'You'd better not turn out to be a spy,' Emily said. 'I'd never live that one down.' She gave him a long sideways look. 'Here, you're not a spy, are you?'

'No,' he said. 'I'm not a spy.'

'Well, I doubt you'd tell me if you was, so I'll just have to take your word for it, won't I?'

''Fraid so!'

'Well, spy or not, you're not to mind.'

'Mind? What am I supposed to be minding?'

'The feather, you daft thing!' Emily slapped his arm, gently – and left her hand resting there. 'No, you're not to mind. What do that lot in there know about the War? Not a thing. Not one thing. None of them are going to get their call-up, are they? All too old. You'd be better sticking Jack Jones's old pig in a uniform and sending that out. Oh, it's easy to be brave sitting with your pals in the Fox all warm and with plenty of beer to hand, isn't it? Not so easy when you're stuck out there in the mud with the fleas and the rats for company.' Emily felt her eyes prickling. She was probably saying too much, but she didn't care. She was past minding her words on account of others. 'Besides, they've got no idea why you're at home, have they? You could have been wounded, couldn't you?'

A sudden, dreadful thought crossed her mind. 'Here, you're not a conchie, are you? Because I'd never live that one down neither.'

'A conchie?' he said. 'What's that?'

She stopped in her tracks. 'A conscientious objector, of course – here, how do you not know that? Where *have* you been?'

'Nowhere, Emily, honestly. I've just… had a lot on my mind recently. But, no – I'm not a conscientious objector.'

'Have you been in the army?'

He hesitated before answering. The moon disappeared behind a cloud and all of a sudden she couldn't make out his features any more, only dark shapes and shadows. 'No,' he said. 'Well, sort of. It's difficult to explain and I can't say any more, Emily… Um. Careless talk costs lives, you know, that kind of thing…'

'You shouldn't say if you don't want to. Don't tell me a lie, though.'

'I'm not a spy, and I'm not a conchie.' The moon came back and again she saw that lop-sided smile, enough to turn a girl soft. 'I don't think I'm a coward either. But you'll have to take my word for that, too.'

'Well,' Emily said gently, 'what sort of world would it be if you couldn't take a young gentleman at his word?' She patted his arm.

'You're a nice lad, aren't you, Mr Williams? You listen. Most lads soon stop listening or never start in the first place. You can tell a good lad by the way he listens. Not much for a girl to ask, is it?' Reaching out, she took the white feather from him and stuck it into her hat, next to the little jet butterfly. 'There,' she said. 'Because we're all in this together, aren't we?'

'Yes,' he said. 'You're right about that.'

The stars twinkled brightly in the unpolluted sky. Emily looked round at the dark fields. She felt all shy herself, now. They weren't so far from the village and she wondered if anyone could see them. 'Oh, I can't stand how long this bloomin' walk takes. Every bloomin' night. Let's take the shortcut.'

Her companion looked doubtfully across the dark field. 'I can't see a path —'

'There is one,' Emily said, 'if you know your way. Don't worry, Mr Williams, I won't drag you into the woods!' She crossed the lane, clambered onto the fence and hopped down the other side. 'I can give you a hand if you need it,' she said, cheekily.

'I *think* I'll manage…' Carefully he climbed onto the fence, and sat on top, legs straddling it. He looked ever so uncomfortable, like a hen perched on top of an unexpectedly large egg.

Emily laughed. 'You have to be a city boy – it's like you've never seen a fence before tonight!'

'Actually, I'm from a village, it's just I'm not usually the one doing the climbing.'

'Got a pal to do it for you?'

'Something like that.' He swung his legs over and jumped down.

'Everyone needs a pal, Mr Williams. I'll be yours if you'll be mine.' She held out her hand, and he took it – and suddenly the laughter bubbled up from inside her like a little brook, the way it used to with her Sam, and Emily broke into a run, pulling her companion after her across the dark field and down into the hollow.

The trees came from nowhere. Mr Williams yanked Emily's arm so hard she came to a sudden halt.

'Ow!' Emily dropped his hand to rub her shoulder. 'Oi! That hurt!'

'Sorry! Sorry! We were getting very close to the trees.'

'The trees? Don't tell me you believe all that nonsense about the woods?'

'The nonsense?'

'Swallow Woods,' she said. 'Haven't you heard – they swallow you up!' She wiggled her fingers spookily. 'Nonsense.'

Williams peered through the branches, as if trying to catch a glimpse of something. 'Don't underestimate old stories,' he said. 'Stories are powerful. And nonsense is sometimes a word for something we don't quite understand, yet.' He looked back towards the lane. 'Perhaps we should keep to the path,' he said, more to himself, it seemed, than to Emily. 'Perhaps we should find out where that takes us. If there's a path, there has to be a *reason* for the path...'

'It's a shortcut. It doesn't go near the woods.' Emily felt put out that he was no longer paying her any attention. All this was spoiling the mood. 'You're not afraid of some bloomin' old trees, are you—?'

'Ssh!' He held his finger up to his lips.

'Don't shush me, Lord Muck!'

'Listen!' he whispered. 'Can you hear it?'

'I can't hear a thing...' He was starting to frighten her. She was painfully aware now that she was alone in a dark field with a complete stranger. But the man didn't make any move to hurt her. He kept on listening for a while, and then shook his head.

'Funny,' he said, to himself again, like she wasn't there. 'If I didn't know better, I'd say it was a motorway...'

'A which-way?'

He turned to her and smiled. 'I'm sorry, Emily,' he said. 'Didn't mean to startle you. I… Oh, don't worry about it. Shall we go back to the path?'

'I don't want to go back to the path,' Emily said. She felt scared now, tricked, as if she had been brought here under false pretences. 'I'm not sure I want to go anywhere with you.'

'OK… Er… Well, we can stand here for a bit… If you'd rather.'

'I'm not sure I want to stand anywhere with you, neither!'

'Then what do you want to do? We'll do whatever you want.' Williams held his hands up, a peace offering. 'I don't want to scare you. I'm not scary, you know. I'm very ordinary.' He looked it too, an ordinary young man completely bewildered as to what he'd done to upset a young lady. Emily suddenly felt very foolish, and very sad. 'What do you want to do, Emily?'

'Oh, I don't know!' Emily cried. Why had she come out here with this young man? What had she been thinking? Everyone had heard her say he could walk her home. She'd be a laughing stock in the morning. But why shouldn't she come here with him? She was twenty years old, and her heart was broken, perhaps beyond repair – and what she wanted most of all was to feel alive again, young again, as young as she'd felt that night two years earlier when Sammy finally plucked up his courage and slipped the ring on her finger. Turning her back on Mr Williams, Emily walked slowly and deliberately towards the trees.

'Emily… Er, what are you doing?'

Emily looked up at the sky. It was cloudy; the moon and the stars were gone. When she looked back over her shoulder, she could no longer see Williams through the dark. Something of her old spirit flared up within her.

'Catch me if you can,' she said and, with a laugh as young as spring water, she ran into Swallow Woods. Behind her, she heard Williams yell, 'Emily! Wait!' An owl, startled by the commotion, flapped up from its branch and hooted out its grievance across the empty silent fields before swooping off, high over the hollow. The two young people passed beneath the trees. Their leaves shuddered, and then turned unnaturally still. And that was the last Amy or the Doctor heard of Rory for quite some time.

Chapter

3

England, now, four days later

The clock on the wall was a perfectly ordinary clock, the kind of clock that could be found in any institutional setting on practically every planet. The planet in question being Earth, this clock displayed (in perfectly ordinary circular fashion) a clear set of numbers ranging from 'one' to 'twelve'. It also had an hour hand, a minute hand, and a second hand which ticked resolutely and didn't lose time in such a way as to make life inconvenient for anyone. All told, this was a perfectly ordinary clock.

The wall upon which the clock hung was also ordinary, and the room of which the wall formed one side wasn't particularly distinguished either. It had four stackable office chairs, a decent-sized table on which sat some recording equipment, a door with a lock, and a window with a view onto a car park. There was a blind on the window, but that was broken, and had been for several weeks. People kept forgetting to write the memo. The blind slumped diagonally down across the window, and was likely to remain in this position for some time yet. People had other things on their mind.

About the only thing that wasn't exactly ordinary about the room was the man sitting behind the table. This man was on the youngish side of indeterminately aged, relatively tall, and he had unkempt hair and two pairs of loose limbs that looked as if they would fit more properly onto an entirely different body. The man wore a nice bow tie and an exasperated expression. He had spent the last forty minutes alternating between drumming his fingers on the table top and swinging back on his chair. About four minutes earlier he had started to get seriously bored.

The door swung open and two detectives walked in (for this ordinary room was one of many that, when put together, comprised a decent-sized if ordinary small-town police station). The man in the bow tie looked up.

'Look,' he said, 'is this going to take much longer? Because the fact is I'm actually on quite a tight schedule and if that clock of yours up there is accurate – and I imagine it's accurate, you all seem like very sober and responsible people, and it seems like a very sober and responsible kind of clock – then I need to go and chase down a couple of young women.'

The two detectives – an older red-haired man, and a younger blonde woman – looked at each other.

'I'm afraid that won't be possible, sir,' said the older one, as he took his seat.

The younger detective sat down next to him and reached across to switch on the recording equipment. 'Interview recommenced at,' she glanced up at the clock, 'ten thirty-seven.'

'You seem to spend a lot of time on the road,' said the older detective. 'Do you travel around with many young women?'

'Ah,' said the unordinary young man. 'Now. I see where you're heading with that question, and I want to make it perfectly clear right away that none of them have ever come along unwillingly. Besides, it's strictly invitation only.' He considered these last statements. 'Well, I suppose there was the history teacher. And the air stewardess. But they both had opportunities to leave and they both decided to stay… I'm not helping myself, am I?'

There was a slight and very strained silence.

'I do need to get going, though,' the young man said. 'Things have turned out not to be as perfectly straightforward as I'd anticipated.'

'Have you ever met a young woman called Laura Brown?'

'No. And I haven't met Vicky Caine either… Oh, you hadn't mentioned her yet, had you? I'm really not helping myself, am I?'

'If there is anything at all that you would like to tell us,' said the older detective, 'now is the time to do it.'

'How about – if you want to find your two missing girls, then you should let me go immediately because you are dealing with a situation way beyond your comprehension? No? No, somehow I didn't think you'd be persuaded. Oh dear, this is going to cause us some difficulties… What can I tell you…? Ah! There is something! Something that's been bothering me.'

The young man put his elbow on the table and leaned forwards, beckoning to the two detectives to come closer. His eyes were very dark, shadowed, and they didn't give anything away. Half-unconsciously, half-unwillingly, both detectives leaned in to listen.

'Somebody,' the young man whispered, 'really ought to fix that blind.'

Two hours later, the police press conference about the two missing girls was getting ready to start. The TV journalists and news reporters had been gathering in the town square for the last hour like crows from a Hitchcock movie. The area directly in front of the police station was packed out; some of the cameramen had resorted to standing on the steps leading up to the war memorial in order to get any pictures at all.

Jess Ashcroft made her way through the crowd, ignoring the complaints of those she passed as she pushed doggedly through. Three or four feet from the front, she stopped, peered over the last few heads and nodded, satisfied that she was close enough to see. Just about. She dumped her bag on the ground, rummaged around, and pulled out a pen and notepad.

'Nice moves,' said a voice in her ear.

Jess looked round. The speaker was a bone-thin young man, expensively clad, holding a mobile phone like it was part of him. She recognised him at once from one of the news channels.

'Big story,' said Jess. 'I don't want to miss anything.'

'Quite right!' He grinned at her. White teeth. Cute as a button. 'I like your style, though.'

'You know what the old song says. Dedication's all you need.'

He laughed. 'Good for you! So, what do you make of the whole thing?'

'Well…' Jess didn't want to play all her cards, not all at once. 'Must be awful for the families, mustn't it?'

'Yes, yes,' he said, rather impatiently, 'but the police kept the first one quiet, didn't they? There's something weird going on there.'

'Laura Brown *is* eighteen years old,' Jess said cagily. 'An adult. Well within her rights to get up and go wherever she likes.'

'Nah…' The TV journalist shook his head. 'Doesn't make sense. She was studying for A levels. Fundraising for a trip to Africa. Not the type to disappear into the blue. Yet the police don't seem to have been bothered until the second one went missing. You have to wonder whether it would have helped poor Vicky Caine if she'd known there was kidnapper on the loose. I think someone's head will roll over this.'

Jess chewed her pen. In fact, it had been

no surprise to her that a second girl had gone missing. She'd been dreading the news ever since her younger sister, Lily, had texted two weeks earlier that her school friend Laura Brown wasn't answering calls and her Facebook page hadn't been updated. Jess had been waiting almost unconsciously to hear who was next.

'Exam pressure?' she said, not believing that for a second. 'It can hit some people hard.'

'Not likely to hit both of them, though, is it? I'm Charlie, by the way.'

'I know. I've seen you on the telly. I'm Jess, from *The Herald*.'

His expression changed from friendly interest to friendly pity. 'Local paper? Bless.'

'It's not *all* cinema listings and fake horoscopes, you know.'

'No, I bet it's not. I bet your octogenarian birthday coverage is first rate.'

'Say what you like, but if anyone's going to get a break on this story, it'll be someone with local knowledge.'

'Someone like you, you mean?'

'Well, why not?'

Charlie laughed. 'Then I'd better stick close to you, Lois Lane.'

'Oh yes, very funny, chuckle chuckle. My kid sister likes that one.'

'Keep your hair on, Lois. We're all in this together.'

'I think it helps to know the town, that's all.'

'Ah, and you're probably right. Hey,' he nudged her, 'eyes forward. Here comes Inspector Knacker of the Yard. Not that he'll have anything new to tell us.'

'You think so?'

'What's he told us so far, Lois? It's his head for the chop, I think. Bet you five quid he won't tell us anything.'

'Fine by me. Because I bet he's going to tell us they've made an arrest.'

'Fighting talk! What gives you that idea?'

Jess tapped her biro against her nose and then pointed the tip of the pen towards the policeman. 'Shush. I want to listen.'

Detective Inspector Galloway waited patiently on the steps while the cameras flashed and a yell of questions leapt up, like the barking of hounds. Jess liked Galloway; she'd interviewed him a couple of times in the eighteen months since his arrival in town from Inverness. She had found him preternaturally polite and unfailingly helpful. Poor man. He looked dog tired, as if he'd been dragged through a ditch and then forced into a suit. The suit looked like it had been having an even worse time.

'I'll be making only a short statement right now,' Galloway said. 'I cannot of course comment on an ongoing investigation.'

'Inspector,' someone called from the crowd, 'there've been some questions as to why the police were so slow in investigating the disappearance of Laura Brown and whether this contributed at all to the disappearance of Vicky Caine. Can you comment on that?'

'I cannot comment,' Galloway said patiently, 'on an ongoing investigation. I shall be reading out a short statement—'

'Inspector,' someone else shouted, 'can you confirm that no searches have as yet been carried out in the woodland area north of the motorway? Can you say why this is the case?'

Galloway hesitated. Jess, watching him, sucked in her breath, sharply. Was he about to go off script? What on *earth* would he say?

But Galloway collected himself. He cleared his throat and started again. 'I'll just read out a short statement,' he said. 'I can confirm that an arrest has been made in connection...' All around the square, cameras began to flash, throwing Galloway briefly off his stride. '...an arrest has been made in connection with the disappearances of Laura Brown and Vicky

Caine. A white male, mid-twenties…' Galloway stopped and blinked into the cameras. 'A white male in his mid-twenties is currently helping us with our enquiries. That's all I can say at the moment.'

The clamour of questions rose up again immediately – *'Inspector, can you confirm that this is now a murder enquiry?* – but Galloway turned and went back into the station.

Jess breathed out. She felt a deep sense of relief, as if some kind of disaster had been narrowly averted. She took off her glasses to rub her eyes.

Beside her, Charlie was opening up his wallet. 'I'm impressed,' he said, handing over a fiver. 'Honestly. And I take back what I said about you being Lois Lane. You're obviously Sherlock Holmes.'

'Hmm.' Jess wiped her specs clean and perched them on her nose again. She peered school-marmishly through them at Charlie. 'Sherlock Holmes was a detective, you know, not a journalist.'

'Lois it is, then.'

'Or you could call me by my name. Which is Jess.'

'Come to the pub, Lois. A gang of us are heading over later to the one on the corner. The

Fantastic Fox —'

'That will be the Fancy Fox.'

'Hey, you really do know everything! Whatever it's called, we'll be there from around seven. Come and meet some people. Get your name about. I promise I won't tell them it's Lois.' He went on his way with a wave. 'See you later!'

Jess bent down to pick up her bag. When she stood up straight again, she found herself staring directly at a stripy scarf. The wearer of the scarf was a young woman clutching a supermarket plastic bag in front of her so tightly that her knuckles had gone white.

'It's Jess, isn't it?' she said. 'You're Jess Ashcroft.'

'I am she, there is no other.'

'Oh, at *last*!' The young woman practically stamped her foot. 'Where have you been hiding? I've been looking for you everywhere! It's not *that* big a town!'

Unobtrusively, Jess manoeuvred her bag between herself and the other woman. 'Wherever I've been, I'm here now.' She glanced around. The crowd was thinning out, but there were still plenty of people around she could call on for help. If all else failed, her bag was heavy, full of junk, and could probably pack a significant punch if swung. 'Is there something I can do to help you, Ms…?'

'My name's Amy. Amy Pond. No, you can't help me – it's you that needs my help.'

'I do?'

'Yes, you really do. You're next, Jess. You're going to disappear next. But don't worry! This time it should all work out OK. This time, I'm coming with you.'

Chapter
4

England, autumn 1917, earlier that afternoon

The TARDIS landed with a groan, like an ancient relative settling down into an armchair after a lengthy lunch. A robin perched on the signpost that pointed down Long Lane towards the mill, tipped its head and studied the blue box with bright inquisitive eyes. The door creaked open. The robin, put out rather than startled, flew away.

Rory Williams – known universally these days as Mr Amy Pond – stepped out of the TARDIS, blinking like an owl in the bright chilly daylight. Nobody else followed him out. Should anyone have been watching – bird, beast, human, other – they would have seen him turn round, as if suddenly in doubt, only to find the way back into the TARDIS entirely and quite mercilessly barred by his new wife and her pet time traveller.

'Look,' Rory said, in the slightly desperate tone someone might use when he knows that a critical moment has arrived but holds out no particular hope that his very real and pressing concerns are going to be heard. 'It's all very well dumping me here in the middle of nowhere, but the last time that happened I ended up waiting thousands of years. Not an exaggeration! Actually thousands! And I was plastic. Plastic! Do you have any idea what it's like, being plastic? Actually plastic!'

'Actually,' said the Doctor, 'that wasn't you.'

'It could have been me! It might still could have been me! Frankly, it's not hard to imagine it being me!'

Amy ruffled his hair. 'Poor Rory,' she said, with perhaps more glee than sympathy. 'You're your very own action figure.'

The Doctor at least had the courtesy to try a more conciliatory line. 'I promise you'll hardly know we're gone. An afternoon's work, that's all. Well, an afternoon and a bit. An afternoon and an evening. Possibly some of tonight as well… What I mean is, it'll all be over by this time tomorrow.' The Doctor thought about that. 'Your time.' He thought some more. 'Ish.'

'Thanks,' said Rory. 'I feel much more confident now.'

'Think of it this way,' Amy said. 'I get to go and visit our own time. Wow. Thrilling. Can't wait. Meanwhile, *you* get to spend a nice afternoon in a country pub. A real historic country pub, while it's actually being historic. So enjoy the moment! Live it up! Feel the vibe! Drink the beer!'

'Eat the pie,' suggested the Doctor. 'It'll be good honest country pie.'

'And there'll be yokels. You can watch them doing… yokel things.'

'Ooh, and you get to chat up a pretty girl,' said the Doctor; seeing Amy's expression, he hastily corrected himself. 'Or not. In fact, I strongly suggest you do absolutely the opposite of that.'

'Yes, yes,' Rory said, 'beer, pie, pub, yokels – it all sounds very nice, and it probably would be, if it wasn't slap bang in the middle of *the war to end all wars—*'

'Oh, that's *miles* away,' the Doctor said breezily.

'That's all very well for you to say!'

'Different country! There's the whole Channel between you.' The Doctor licked the tip of his forefinger and held it aloft, testing the air. 'Nope, no Zeppelins. Not today. Zip. Nada. No show. Absolutely nothing to worry about! Besides, you'll barely know you were here. These short trips are like bread and butter to the TARDIS. Quick turn of a dial, quick pull of a lever; we're in, we're out, we… um, shake it all about… Yes, well, as I say, nothing to worry about.' He waggled his finger and adopted a lecturing voice. 'What you need to be concentrating on is staying close to Emily Bostock. Don't let her out of your sight.' He dropped the playfulness and went on in a much quieter, much more serious tone. 'What you're doing is critical, Rory. You have to stay close to her. If we lose Emily, we're right back where we started. More importantly, she'll be gone – *really* gone. I might not be able to get her back.'

'I understand,' Rory said. 'Stay close to Emily Bostock.'

The Doctor gave him a kindly smile. 'You'll be fine. Honestly. Afternoon's work. In the pub. With pie.'

'Don't get *too* close to Emily Bostock, mind,' Amy said. 'You're a married man now. And I'll *know*.' She blew Rory an extravagant kiss, gave him a cheery wave, and closed the TARDIS door.

Rory stepped back to watch the dematerialisation.

The TARDIS, however, robustly carried on being there. After a moment, the door opened again and the Doctor stepped out. He had something cupped between his hands and a somewhat sheepish expression on his face. He sidled up to Rory.

'One last thing.' He opened his hands to reveal a small triangular device made from some bronze substance that definitely wasn't bronze. He pressed it into Rory's palm. 'You might want to take this.'

The object pulsed and hummed quietly, as if chatting to itself. Gold specks of light sparkled up and down one flat side like tiny Christmas tree lights. The other side was smooth and blank.

Rory said, 'This is the thing that lets you find me again, isn't it?'

'Um.'

'By "um", you mean "Yes, Rory", don't you, Doctor?'

'Ah.'

'And by "ah", you mean "I'm sorrier than I can possibly say, Rory". *Don't* you, Doctor?'

'Rory, everything's fine. Go to the pub. Chat to Emily,' the Doctor glanced quickly back over his shoulder, 'in an entirely platonic fashion. Keep her close, and keep *that*,' he tapped the bronze triangle, 'with you at all times. When you get where you're going, press that button on the edge there – no, the other edge – and we'll be with you in the blink of an eye.' He closed Rory's hand over the device. 'And when you do go into the woods – *concentrate*. There's nothing there that can hurt you, but you might get disorientated. Don't worry about that. The most important thing is that you don't let Emily out of your sight.' Again, the Doctor gave his kindly, ancient smile, the one that you could only feel proud to get, because it meant someone very wise and very special trusted you beyond measure. Rory couldn't help but be pleased to receive that smile.

'We'll be back before you know we're gone,' the Doctor said, which turned out to be completely true, in a manner of speaking. With one last vast grin, the Doctor loped back inside the TARDIS. Soon the old time machine was grumbling and groaning again, and then it was gone.

From his pocket, Rory pulled out a scruffy scrap of paper onto which a map had been scribbled. Emily Bostock worked as a barmaid at a pub called the Fox. The pub stood at a crossroads opposite an old mill. Slowly, Rory's gaze drifted up from the map to the signpost at the corner of the lane. *Brown's Mill*, it told him helpfully. *3½ miles*. Rory burst out laughing.

'Bang on as ever! Thanks, Doctor!'

He shoved the map back into his pocket and set off down the lane. Soon he was whistling, because the day was perfect for walking, the trees green and gold, and the sun not too hot, and there was the promise of a pint at the end. Altogether, this struck Rory as not a bad deal, and almost certainly better than being plastic. Some pleasures stay much the same, whatever the time and place. Trouble, however, comes in many different shapes and sizes.

Chapter
5

England, now, after the press conference

Detective Inspector Gordon Galloway had never intended to live amongst the barbarians. Then, on a walking holiday in the Lake District, he fell in love, his eyes meeting the intriguingly green ones of his wife-to-be over a full English breakfast in a pleasant B&B near Lake Coniston. Nearly the first thing Mary said to him was, 'I'm something of a home bird…' And so – after eleven months, a charming courtship, and a delightful wedding – Gordon Galloway applied for, and received, a transfer to his wife's home town.

A town which, after eighteen months of everyday living and slightly over a week into his first major case there, Galloway was concluding was a very strange town indeed.

It wasn't simply that Laura Brown's disappearance had gone unreported for several days. Parents know their children, after all, and technically Laura Brown was an adult. If she had decided to pack up and take an early gap year, that was her decision, and if her parents had assumed that was what she had done, that was theirs. And as soon as it was clear that something else was happening (when Vicky Caine's frantic and Scouse father turned up at the station to report the non-appearance of his daughter), the Brown family had become as accommodating (and as frightened) as Galloway might have expected.

No, he didn't suspect the Browns, not least because of the strength of their alibis. But there was still something strange. Take that moment earlier today, when he had gone to inform both sets of parents that he had made an arrest, and Laura's mother and father – Vicky's mother too – had stared at him as if he had said he was planning to search the dark side of the moon. It was as if the three of them couldn't quite believe what he was saying.

Vicky's father – who wasn't local, after all – had reacted more as Galloway had expected:

Who is it? Do we know him? How did you catch up with him? Then the other three had joined in – but it still hung there, that split second, when they had all stared at each other, clearly all thinking the same thing: *How can that be possible?* Yes, much as it pained him even to think it (for Gordon Galloway was very much in love with his wife) there was something very strange about this town.

Then there was the not so inconsiderable matter of the searches. Vicky Caine's last known location was a bus stop on Long Lane. Laura Brown had last been seen leaving the Fancy Fox pub. Between these two points lay a large piece of woodland. Galloway had several times ordered a search, but somehow it didn't seem to happen. People found themselves elsewhere, or something pressing turned up, or the searchlights were broken and had to be replaced. Each delay was perfectly reasonable. But the upshot was that the search of Swallow Woods had not yet got started.

And then there was the chief suspect…

Galloway glanced across his desk to where his junior colleague, DC Ruby Porter, was talking on the phone. Porter was a pensive young woman that even Galloway thought was slightly too sensible for her age. He went and made them both a cup of coffee. By the time he got back, she had finished her call, and they sat sipping hot instant stuff from nearly clean mugs.

'Tell me,' said Galloway, 'do you think we have the right man?'

'Absolutely.'

'Why do you think that?'

'Um. Intuition?'

'Go on, you can do better than that!'

Porter peered at him over the rim of her mug. 'I don't want to sound strange, sir.'

Strange. There was that word again. 'Hm. Don't worry about that. Fire ahead. Then I'll tell you what I think.'

'OK… Well, it's not the hair, and it's not the clothes… I don't know, but when we're in there talking to him, sometimes he looks at me, and it's like…'

'Go on,' Galloway prompted.

'It's like he's the oldest person I've ever met. There's the word games, and the chatter, and the nonsense, but sometimes I catch him looking straight at me, and when I look into his eyes, deep into his eyes, it's like I'm staring all the way back to the beginning of time.'

There was a pause. If Galloway had had an audience to his earlier thoughts, he would now have turned round to them and said: *See! See what I mean? This town is strange!* As it was, he simply swirled some coffee around his mouth and then swallowed.

'That's… very poetic, Porter. See, I was only going to say that it was extremely odd that there's no evidence of him being in town until right before Laura Brown went missing.'

Porter turned an interesting shade of red. 'Sorry, sir. But it's the only way I can think of putting it. He seems harmless, but if I think about it at all, he might well be the strangest person I've ever met.'

And coming from someone brought up in this town, *that*, Galloway thought, was practically a testimonial.

They finished their lousy coffee and went back down to the interview room. Opening the door, Galloway saw that his chief suspect was standing by the wall, staring at the clock. When he heard the door open, the young man pointed up at it.

'Is that accurate?' he said. 'Are you quite sure it's accurate?'

'Of course it is. Why don't you sit down, son?'

The young man sat down, slowly. Then, with a quick movement, he reached out and grabbed

Galloway's wrist. Porter's hand flashed out to stop him, but the young man said, 'Stop. *Wait.*'

And for some reason she did. The three of them sat there, motionless as a tableau, all staring down at Galloway's watch. The second hand ticked on, on, on, and each second seemed to have slowed, to be taking an age. And then at last it reached the hour. The young man, looking up, stared straight at Galloway – who, all of a sudden, could see what Porter meant. It nearly scared the life out of him.

'It's time,' said the strange young man with the madcap hair and the clownish bow tie and the fathomless eyes. 'Amy and Jess. It's time.'

Chapter
6

England, now, the Fancy Fox pub,
shortly before 7 p.m.

Jess got to the Fox early. She claimed the big table to the right-hand side of the pub, dumping her leather bag on it to mark the territory as taken. She got a gin and tonic, and then sat checking her text messages, hoping she looked busy rather than worriedly waiting for a group of people who might not turn up. One of her messages was from her sister, Lily:

An ARREST?!!!? Wots this all about, LOIS? Any news on Luara? :-(

Jess was in the middle of a lengthy reply (Jess made no concessions to the form: her text messages contained full sentences, accurate punctuation, and no missing or misplaced apostrophes – she would also manage to spell 'Laura' correctly), when she realised that someone was sitting at the table.

'I'm really sorry,' she said, adding the last full stop and hitting *send*, 'those seats are taken— Oh. It's you.'

For it was indeed the alarming Amy Pond, clutching her plastic bag as if it bore a designer label. 'Don't run off again,' she said. 'We don't have time, OK?'

'Please leave me alone,' Jess said, in a clear and carrying voice. A couple of the other patrons looked round curiously, decided Jess could handle herself for the moment, and went back to their drinks and conversations.

'Look, OK, all right, I know we got off on the wrong foot—'

'You practically *threatened* me!'

'—but it's really important you hear what I have to say.'

The pub doors swung open. With a gale of laughter, Charlie and his friends entered the Fox. Through clenched teeth, Jess hissed, 'You are about to ruin what could be the most important moment in my career.'

'*This*,' Amy hissed back, 'is the most important moment in your career. Story of your life, Jess.

Happening now, whether you like it or not.'

Charlie, who had ordered at the bar and was looking round, saw Jess. He grinned dashingly and waved.

'I want you to go away now,' Jess said.

'It's about the woods, Jess. Swallow Woods.'

Jess's heart stopped, gulped, then started again. 'The woods?' she whispered. 'What about them? What do you know?'

'I know an awful lot about them – not everything, but a lot. The rest we'll have to find out as we're going along.' Amy stood up. She smiled, rather grimly. 'Oh, you're *so* coming with me.'

Jess glanced across at Charlie, who was now trying to pick up four pint glasses. 'Tomorrow,' she promised. 'Come and see me at *The Herald* tomorrow.'

Jess had never actually seen someone tear at their hair before. Now she had.

'Aren't you *listening*? Tomorrow? It's now or never!'

Charlie arrived with his friends and his tower of drinks, and set the glasses carefully down on the table. The introductions went round. Charlie smiled at Amy, towering and glowering over Jess.

'Hi!' he said. 'Friend of yours, Jess?'

'Not exactly…'

'Oh…' His ears almost twitched. 'A lead?'

Story of your life, Amy mouthed at Jess – and Jess knew she couldn't resist. She pushed her specs back up her nose and beamed guilelessly at Charlie. 'Eighty-fourth birthday party,' she lied. 'Twins. Big story for me. Huge. But I'll come back later and tell you your horoscope.'

'We'll be here, Lois. We'll cross your palm with silver and then you can buy the beer.'

'I'll be five minutes,' Jess promised. 'Um. Maybe ten.'

Amy marched Jess over to a table in a quieter corner of the pub, glaring at the man already sitting there until he got up and left.

'You are very strange,' Jess remarked, as Amy started emptying the contents of the plastic bag onto the table. Piles of printouts and photographs.

'I don't have time not to be strange,' Amy said. She sifted through some of the photographs and made a selection. 'Right. Best place to start is probably with the aerial shots – hoo boy, did they ever creep me out! – yes, we'll start with those.' She handed one of the photographs to Jess.

Jess put the photo down on the table and

studied it. As Amy had said, it was an aerial shot of a piece of countryside. A thick dark smudge of woodland took up most of the centre of the picture. Curving around the woods, at the bottom right-hand side of the page, was a strip of grey road. The town took up the left-hand vertical strip of the page. It was very familiar.

'That's Swallow Woods.' Amy jabbed her finger at the dark green patch. 'And *that*,' she ran her finger along the grey road, 'is the motorway.'

'I know,' said Jess, patiently. 'I've lived round here my whole life—'

'So don't tell me you've never noticed.'

'Noticed what?'

'The *road*, Jess! The motorway!'

'What about the motorway? It's a stretch of motorway. It runs from Junction 11 with the bypass down *here*,' Jess pointed to a place on the table just below the bottom left corner of the picture, then swept her finger up and round to a point just above the right corner, 'to Junction 12 *here*. Both junctions get backed up at rush hour. It's a pain in the neck. I write about it every three or four months and nothing changes. Why? Because it's a perfectly ordinary piece of motorway—'

'Did you not see what your hand just did?'

Amy said. 'The *shape* it made?'

'If you've got something to tell me, get on with it. Because right now I could be networking my way into a job in London—'

Amy shook her head. 'You're not going. You won't leave here.'

'Once again, that sounds unpleasantly like a threat—'

'Look at the *road*,' Amy said. She pulled out another picture, another aerial shot of trees and field and road, and then a third picture. Jess shook her head, but she examined them both. There was no new town in these – only the old village, more or less where they were sitting now – and certainly no motorway – although the old road was there, following broadly the same route. But the shape of the woods was unmistakeable. These were aerial shots of the same piece of countryside, over time.

'Look at the roads, Jess,' Amy urged softly. 'They *bend*. They bend around the woods.' She lined the three pictures up alongside each other, and pointed to the one on the far right. 'That's the road the Romans built. They built it on top of the old trackway.'

'Whoa, whoa, whoa – hang on a minute! The *Roman* road?'

Jess grabbed the picture. This road wasn't a

trace, a memory, the bumps and indentations that get left behind and overgrown, the kind of thing that gets Tony Robinson excited on *Time Team*. This was a road – a working road. A road in use. 'This looks like the *actual* Roman road.'

'It is the actual Roman road. You may remember,' Amy said, 'that Roman roads are famous for being straight, unless they've got a very good reason not to be. And you may notice that this one isn't straight. At all.'

She was right too. At the point where the Roman road met what Jess, in her time, would call Long Lane, it took a sharp south-easterly swing. Eventually, where Junction 12 was now, it righted itself, carrying on its steady north-easterly progress. Jess could see how the road could have been straight. But it wasn't straight. It bypassed the woods.

'That isn't the best one,' Amy said. 'Oh no, no sirree! *This*,' she pulled out another picture, 'is the one that really got me going.'

She handed Jess the picture. This time, the road was a narrow brown line. But it followed the same path, and it curved in exactly the same way. It curved to keep away from cutting through the woods.

'Look at the pictures, Jess,' Amy said softly. 'The motorway bends around the woods. So did the old road. So did the Roman road. As long as people have lived here, they've gone out of their way to avoid the woods. That,' she pointed to the thin brown line on the third picture, 'is the trackway. It's Bronze Age. And it bends away from Swallow Woods.'

Jess sat with the Roman photo in one hand, the Bronze Age one in the other, staring between them.

'This picture,' Jess said slowly, holding up the one showing the trackway, 'looks like it was taken yesterday.'

'Sometime last week, actually,' Amy said. 'Or six thousand years ago, depending on how you look at it.'

'Oh, now you're just being ridiculous!'

'Jess.' Amy put her hand upon her arm. 'You've lived here your whole life. You know this town better than most. You know there's something strange about Swallow Woods.'

Jess licked her lips. 'They're just stories. The kind of thing you tell to kids to stop them wandering off by themselves...'

'Yet when I said I wanted to talk about the woods, you came at once. Those guys over there, you could be chatting away to them right now! Fixing up that fancy London job you've always wanted. But you aren't. You're here with me. Because you want to know the secret of Swallow Woods. All your life, Jess. All your life you've been wondering.' Amy started sifting through her papers again. 'You know that people go missing. That the woods swallow them. Not just Laura, not just Vicky – it's been going on much longer than that. If you look into it, just a day's work, you soon find out that people have been disappearing in Swallow Woods for as long as people have been living here. The trackway, Jess. It bends away from the woods. Those Bronze Age people, they knew. Everyone who's lived here, they've known. Because there's a pattern. Every fifty years it happens, give or take a couple of years. Take a look at these.'

She handed Jess a sheaf of papers: old newspaper reports, from the nineteenth century and earlier. Before that was a selection of parish records, the steady rise and fall of births and deaths across the centuries – but when Jess looked closely at the records, she saw that some of the names had no death date, and that each of these had a green mark against them. Whatever the century, the same mark. Different hands, but the same mark; young men and young women, but the same mark. 1917 – two marks. 1861 – three marks. 1814 – one mark.

At the bottom of the pile was the entry in the Domesday Book. There was the parish – St Jude's – and there was the entry for the wood. Someone had carefully cross-hatched through the name. Nobody wanted to own Swallow Woods. Nobody would go near it.

Jess shoved the papers away. 'You've done all this on a computer – I don't know why, but you must have.'

'All right. There's another thing I have to show you,' Amy said. 'I think this will convince you. But you're not going to like it, and I think you should prepare yourself for a shock.' Reaching into the bag, she drew out one last piece of paper.

It was the cover page of a national newspaper. The paper was yellowing and slightly crisp to touch. Jess guessed it was probably a few decades old. She read the headline – *Third Girl Missing* – and then the start of the story beneath. One paragraph had been circled in felt-tip pen: *And with no news on either Laura Brown or Vicky Caine, fears are now mounting for 24-year-old journalist Jess Ashcroft, whose abandoned car was found parked on a country lane…*

'I'm sorry,' Amy said quietly. 'I didn't want to have to show you that. But you have to understand, Jess – I know that you go into

Swallow Woods tonight. I know that you're the next to disappear. There's nothing I can do about that. As far as I'm concerned, you've already gone. But this time – I'm going with you.'

The paper, naturally, was dated tomorrow.

Chapter

7

England, autumn 1917, well after closing time

Rory crashed through the trees. 'Emily! Where are you?' He stopped to catch his breath, bending over, his hands splayed out flat on his legs. 'One job,' he mumbled to himself. 'One. Stay close to Emily Bostock. The Doctor's going to kill me. *Amy*'s going to kill me…'

He felt something small and hard bounce off the back of his head. 'Ow!' Again – and then a third time. A muffled laugh came from above. Emily was perched up in the tree, legs dangling down, weighing one last pine cone like a cricket ball. She had taken off her hat, and loosened her long brown hair. It gleamed in the sunshine. She threw the cone at Rory. He fumbled the catch and it fell to the ground.

'All right,' he said. 'You've had your fun! Are you coming down?'

'Why should I come down? It's nice up here.' She patted the branch next to her. 'Why don't you come up instead?'

Why not? At least she wouldn't be able to run away from him again. Rory grabbed an outlying branch and swung himself up beside her.

'See?' she said. 'Isn't it nice?'

'Oh, yes. Lovely.'

'You don't sound like you mean that, Mr Williams. Here, you're not cross with me, are you?'

'No, it is lovely, just… Please, Em- Miss Bostock, I mean. Please don't run off again like that.'

'Gave you a turn, did I?' She patted his hand. 'All right, I won't run off like that again.'

'Thank you, Miss Bostock.'

'Emily will do.'

'Thank you, Emily.'

They sat for a while, each giving the other quick sideways glances, and then looking hurriedly away.

'They're stories, nothing more,' Emily said at last, apologetically. 'I know we're off the beaten track in Foxton, Mr Williams, but even we're in the twentieth century now! Mr Blakeley up at the big house – his son has a motor car! I've seen it!' She swung her legs to and fro. 'It wasn't working, mind. Slid off into a ditch. The steam that was coming up from it!' She laughed. 'Mind you, they're beautiful things. Imagine what it must feel like, speeding along, the wind in your hair…'

'Maybe one day you'll ride in one.'

'Who, me? I shouldn't think so. Nothing exciting happens here. A motor car might be real enough, but nothing happens in Swallow Woods.'

Rory gave her a sad smile. 'But it's already happening. Haven't you noticed?'

'What do you mean?'

'Look around. What can you see?'

'Trees. We're sitting in a tree looking at more trees.'

'Try again,' Rory said. 'Describe exactly what you can see.'

'Well, where there's trees, there's leaves. I can see leaves. Lots of leaves.'

'Go on.'

'There's a little path heading off just in front of us. I think I can hear a stream, up ahead somewhere. And there's the sun, scattered through the breaks between the branches. It's not such a dense old wood as people would have you think—'

'What time did we leave the Fox, Emily?'

'Just after closing time, of course. That's half past nine.'

'Half past nine. And yet there's the sun. When we left the Fox, the moon was out. Remember? It was nearly full. And now...' Rory waved his hand around. 'Sunshine.'

'So? So the sun's coming up. That happens, you know, even in Foxton. Nothing strange about that.'

'But it's autumn. The nights are longer. How long since we left the pub? An hour at most. How can the sun be coming up already?'

Emily drew her shawl around herself more tightly. 'I don't mind saying so, but you're frightening me, Mr Williams.'

'It's OK,' Rory said softly. 'We're not in any danger, not in any real danger. But Emily – please, promise me, don't run off like that again. Because I might not be able to find you, and if you get lost, you could be lost for ever.'

Emily pulled away from him. In a whisper, she said, 'Who are you, exactly?'

Rory Williams thought of himself as possibly the least alarming person of his acquaintance.

Amy – now *she* was alarming. Gorgeous, wonderful, unique – and alarming. And as for the Doctor… Now Rory saw himself through Emily's eyes: a stranger who appeared from nowhere saying bizarre things while the world went suddenly mad… He knew exactly how it felt to be on the receiving end. He reached out to take Emily's hand. It had gone cold, so he started to rub it.

'Who I am doesn't matter, not really,' he said. 'But it's possible that things are going to get weird around here, Emily, weirder than they are already. It's important that you trust me. I'm a friend. I can look after you.'

As he spoke, the sun shone more brightly on Swallow Woods, catching on the dust motes and pollen and dandelion parachutes that were drifting about, making them gleam for the merest second and then disappear. The leaves were gently stirring. It seemed to Rory almost as if they were held in some eternal Maytime – only Emily's hand was still cold.

'All right, Mr Williams,' she said slowly. 'I'll trust you. But you have to tell me what's going on around here. I'm not daft, and you don't have to lie to me, not even to protect me. You shouldn't do that, not if you want me to trust you. Besides,' she said, and gave him a secretive sideways look, 'we all know about the woods. We pretend it's not real, but we all know about it. So what's happening? What's going on?'

'OK. It's difficult, but try this. Ages ago, someone abandoned a machine in the woods. It's been leaking a kind of energy ever since, like the steam from Mr Blakeley's car, and it's made the woods bend out of shape. That's why all these strange things happen – how it can hop from autumn to summer, or day to night.'

'And why the people... well, why they go missing.'

'Yes, that too. It's not magic or enchantment or anything—'

'Well, I know that! Good gracious, this is the twentieth century! I'm not some simple country girl! I was at school all the way up to 13, I'll have you know!'

'Sorry! Yes, of course, twentieth century... Anyway, this machine has been sitting here rotting and the stuff it's made from makes the strange things happen—'

'Like if Mr Blakeley's motor car broke down near a stream, and some metal got into the water so it turned a funny colour and you couldn't drink it without getting sick?'

'That's.... pretty much exactly what I mean.'

'See – not so daft, am I? Is that why you're

here? To fix the machine?'

'Not so much fix it as find it and cart if off for scrap.'

'And then Swallow Woods will go back to being ordinary?'

'That's the idea.'

Emily rested her hand flat against the trunk of the old tree supporting them. 'Poor old Swallow Woods. Everyone scared, and it's not its fault. Seems a shame to take the magic away, even if it wasn't really magic in the first place.' She stroked the crusty bark with her thumb and sighed. 'Suppose it happens to all of us in time.'

She shook herself and, with a quicksilver movement, slid down from the tree. 'And you knew I came through Swallow Woods and you were worried I'd get lost too. That's nice. I thought you were nice, Mr Williams.' She pulled back her hair and set her hat upon her head, shoving a pin in here and there to keep it fixed in place. Then she put the feather and the butterfly straight.

'Can I help?' she said. 'Help you find the machine?'

Rory clambered down the tree. 'Of course. But we have to stay together.'

'So where now?' she said, when he was on

the ground again. 'Where are we heading?'

'What do you think, Emily?'

'Me? What do I know? Don't you have a map or something?'

'How would you map a place like this? Who would come here to map it?'

She shivered, even in the sunshine. 'You're not helping with my nerves, you know. Well,' she pointed at the path, 'I suppose that's as good a way as any.'

So they went that way, and Rory's heart was heavy, because he had not told Emily everything, not quite. Rory knew that Emily Bostock was going to disappear into Swallow Woods tonight. That's what history said: a green mark against her name in the parish records, one of many marks he and Amy and the Doctor had found leading back through time. Rory's job tonight was to follow Emily, not to lead her; to stay close, to find out where she was going and where she had gone – and perhaps, that way, to save her.

England, 1917, much further from the pub than was intended, early in the afternoon, before the TARDIS left

Amy watched on the monitor as Rory got his

bearings. Then the TARDIS dematerialised, and she could see nothing beyond the formless, timeless Vortex. 'He will be all right, won't he? Doctor?'

'Hmm?' The Doctor was busy tinkering with another small bronze triangular device, exactly the same as the one he had just given Rory.

'Rory. He'll be all right, won't he?'

'Of course he'll be all right. Rory's a trooper. Trooper Rory. Solid as a rock – and not one of those porous rocks that lets water through. Trooper Rory the non-porous rock, that's what they call him.'

'Those woods, though. They sound creepy. Paths moving and shifting and wandering about…'

'It's not going to be a walk in the park, Amy, no, but it is a perfectly normal side effect of this particular kind of interstellar drive. There can be some disorientation at first, but you soon get used to it. We know from the records that Emily disappears, which means she must find her way to the ship eventually. All Rory has to do is stick with her, and then use *this* –' he threw the device to Amy – 'to signal us so that we can get a fix.'

She twisted the triangular object around between her fingers. 'Looks like a piece of —'

'In *no* way,' said the Doctor firmly, 'does my superbly engineered triangular tracking technology resemble a piece of chocolate. And I certainly wouldn't advise biting into it. It may be good for locating people stuck in spatial warps, but I doubt it's good for your fillings.'

'Fillings? Speak for yourself, mister! I looked after my teeth. Brushed *and* flossed. So this little hoojamaflip is really how we're going to find Rory?'

'When he's found the ship, yes.'

'And the reason we can't land the TARDIS right in the woods is because of the temporal wotsit.'

'On this occasion the wotsit is in fact spatial rather than temporal. Swallow Woods is… well, it's bigger on the inside. And the word you're looking for is warp.'

'Warp,' said Amy. 'OK. I'm with you. Nearly. Run it past me again.'

'Pass me your scarf,' said the Doctor.

'Sorry?'

'Your scarf. That's the woollen thing wrapped around your neck.'

'Oi. Watch it.' Amy undid her scarf and handed it over. It was a good scarf, long and thin and with cheerful bright stripes, and Amy was fond of it. 'You're not going to Doctor it, are you? I want it back. Undoctored.'

'I'm not going to do anything to it. Nothing that I wouldn't do to a scarf of my own. Now, watch and listen.' He pulled the scarf out lengthways and held it in front of him. 'About ten thousand years ago – give or take a few thousand years – somebody landed their exploration ship near Swallow Woods. Crash-landed, I should say. Because the ship broke down.'

'And the AA hadn't been invented yet.'

'That's right. No AA. Not for a while. Terrible time. Unspeakable. Now, the cause of the breakdown was that the ship's propulsion unit malfunctioned.'

'Propulsion unit. Is that Doctor for "engine"?'

'Yes, that's Doctor for engine. A thing that gets you from A to B.'

'I call that a cup of tea.'

Calmly, the Doctor said, 'I can hold on to this scarf indefinitely, you know.'

'All right, all right! I'm listening now. Properly.'

'Good. Now, what you must understand about space, Amy, if you haven't worked this out already, is that it's very big. And if you're serious about getting from A to B, you need something considerably more complex than a nice hot cup of tea. You're not trying to move yourself from the kitchen to the sofa. You're trying to span the vast empty spaces that lie between the lonely distant stars. So how do you do that? In the case of our exploration ship, the propulsion unit – engine – folds pieces of space together.'

'I'm guessing my scarf's about to have its moment of glory.'

'Correct.' The Doctor folded the ends of the scarf together, so that a long loop hung down. 'But you can see how all that space gets pushed somewhere, into a sort of pocket. When the ship broke down, the pilot dumped it in Swallow Woods, where it's been causing havoc ever since.' He tugged the scarf so that the loop swung backwards and forwards. 'This is why people disappear. They're caught in these pockets and can't get back out.'

'So if we took the TARDIS into the woods, it would probably get pulled into one of these pockets too. We'd be as lost as anyone else.'

'Exactly. But what we *can* do is follow a couple of missing people from different times, triangulate back from them to work out the position of the ship, remove the broken propulsion unit, and –' he pulled his hands apart and the scarf went straight – 'escort anyone lost back to their own time. It's a perfectly simple clean-up job. I only wish people wouldn't go around fly-tipping. I'm not a cosmic bin man.'

'Do we know where the ship came from, Doctor?'

'I think so.' Slowly, he began to fold the scarf. 'All a long time ago, though. Sad story. Shouldn't dwell on these things.'

'Keep Buggering On, like Winston said, eh?'

'Always, Pond. Always.'

Amy turned her attention back to the bronze device. 'Tracking people through spatial wotsits. Chocolate definitely can't do that.'

'And then there's the nuts and the nougat. Think of your fillings.'

'I don't *have* any— Oh, shut up! What do you call this locator thingie, anyway?'

'Do you know, I hadn't decided on a name.' He peered at it. 'It's triangular and it triangulates. How about we call it a triangulator? Or is that too obvious? No, let's keep things self-explanatory.' He smiled. 'Would you like your scarf back now, Amy? We've landed, and it's autumn.'

Arm-in-arm, Rory and Emily walked through Swallow Woods. The day – if indeed a single day was happening around them – became warmer and sunnier, as if spring was accelerating towards summer. The birdsong grew louder and more joyous. Rory even thought he could hear the leaves unfurling, a gentle steady rising sound. He didn't feel afraid, more awed at the strange swift transformation taking place around him; at the sense of being very close to living things and yet very far away from anything human. Except Emily, of course. She walked through the woods with her mouth open and her eyes bright, seeming to savour every moment of this rapidly passing spring.

After what might have been an hour (both their watches had long since stopped), the trees moved apart, forming a round glade. Entering, they both gasped and fell silent. It was as if they had walked into a vast cathedral, but one that was living and growing, not made of stone. The trees were huge and thick with dark green foliage; their upper branches were interwoven, joining each tree to its neighbour and thereby forming massive archways through which dark avenues leading out from the clearing could be glimpsed. The air was hushed, as if a service was about to begin in an ancient green temple.

'Emily,' Rory whispered. 'Why are you humming?'

'Humming? Wouldn't dare! Be like whistling in church! There's water over there, though. Must be that you can hear.'

A small pool, deep and still, lay at the heart of the clearing. They knelt side-by-side and drank thirstily. Emily splashed water over her face and hands. When the ripples settled, Rory could see their reflections, slightly distorted, and framed by the tall trees.

'Here, what's that?' Emily said. Rory, investigating where she had pointed, found the remains of a campfire; a few charred sticks and some small bones left over from a lonely sort of supper.

'I wonder who else could be here?' Rory said.

'Could be Harry.'

'Harry?'

'Harry Thompson from Brook's Farm. Haven't seen him in the Fox for nigh on six weeks. Word is he's run off. His call-up was due. Poor lamb, he's a sensitive sort. If the trees have been playing tricks on him, he'll be scared half out of his skin.'

Rory picked up one of the burnt sticks and stirred the ashes. They were cold and dead. 'What would you do,' he said, 'if we found him?'

'What would I do? I'd come back here tomorrow with a loaf of bread and a packet of fags and whatever else he asked for. I wouldn't send anyone out to France, not for all the tea in China. They wouldn't send him now, anyway. He's as good as deserted. They shoot you for that.' She stood up, abruptly, brushing away the leaves and twigs and ashes sticking to her long skirt. In a quiet, fierce voice, she said, 'I hope Harry's here. I hope he's all right. I hope he stays here as long as this terrible, evil war goes on.'

'I hope so too, Emily.'

Rory brushed the cinders from his hands and stood up. Emily was humming again – no, that hadn't been her, had it... Before Rory could explore this thought further, Emily reached over, took hold of his chin, and kissed him firmly.

'Ah!' Rory squawked, when he had possession of his own mouth again. 'Yes! No! I'm married!'

Emily stared at him. Her pupils were wide and dark.

'*Married?*'

Somehow, she made the word sound like an accusation. She raised her hand and slapped Rory hard across the cheek. Then she turned and ran beneath one of the arches formed by the trees.

Rory came to his senses. 'Emily! Wait!' He dashed after her along the path, stumbling in his haste. Was it his imagination, or were the roots of the trees hindering him, slowing him? Soon the path forked. Rory came to a halt and looked desperately first one way, then the other. No sign of Emily – but on the ground lay a single white feather.

'Emily!' Rory cried. He wasn't meant to lose her. He wasn't meant to lose her...

Paralysed by indecision, unsure which way to go, Rory rubbed anxiously at his temples. The trees shifted, and scorching sunlight poured through the gaps between them. Rory's eyes blurred and watered. Again he heard humming – no, not humming, not Emily, and not the water in the pool either, which had been still water and not running... The noise grew louder, more a throb or a thrum, and Rory realised that it was mechanical, as unlike birdsong or the gentle rustle of leaves as it was possible for something to be. Dark patches appeared in his vision. The trees began to spin around him. Everything began to ebb away.

I wasn't meant to lose her...

Chapter

8

England, now, slightly before closing time

'Don't say anything,' said Amy. 'I'm not quite finished yet.' From the bag, she pulled out one last aerial photograph. She offered it to Jess, who took it with shaking hands.

Only from the grey line of motorway could Jess tell that this was the same area of countryside that she had seen in the other pictures; her part of the world, and generations of her family before her. Any other continuity with the past had been obliterated. All the houses – the 1930s villas, the 1960s estate, the new estate – they were all gone. In their place were empty fields. And where Swallow Woods had been there was a lake.

'Before you ask,' said Amy, 'this was taken fifty years from now. Yes, in the future. And no – I don't know what happens. I *do* know that it happens over the next few days. You're the last to disappear, Jess. Nobody disappears after you, because there isn't a town for them to disappear from, and there isn't a wood for them to disappear into.'

It seemed to Jess that the everyday sounds of the pub – the laughter, the chatter, the chink of glasses, the cheesy tinkle of the quiz machine – were now coming from a great distance. Blood throbbed in her ears.

'These are fakes,' she said. 'It's easy to fake this kind of thing if you know how.'

'Why?' Amy sounded genuinely baffled. 'Why would I do that?'

'Some kind of hoax—'

'Why bother?'

'A grudge, then. Did I go through a red light while you were on a pedestrian crossing? Did I walk past you and not buy a *Big Issue*? Whatever it was, I'm sorry. I didn't mean it, and I'm sorry. But to do something like *this*...' She crumpled up the newspaper cutting. 'It's cruel!'

'I wouldn't do that,' said Amy. 'For one thing, like I keep saying, I really don't have the time right now! Besides, all this I've shown you –

I'm not telling you anything you didn't already know. But you've been denying it. The whole town has been in denial, for centuries. You, your friends, your parents, your grandparents – you've gone out of your way to avoid Swallow Woods. You've only built roads that keep a safe distance. Think of the council meetings, Jess! The planning permission committees! Everyone there, with the same thought in mind, none of them ever saying it out loud – *we mustn't get too close to the woods...*'

Amy picked up some of the papers, flicked through them. 'Back and back, through the centuries, all your ancestors, for as long as they've lived here, they've all thought the very same thing – *we mustn't get too close to the woods.* Why? Why would they think that? *Centuries,* Jess.'

Jess looked unhappily across the pub. Charlie was still there with his friends. They looked happy and untroubled and as if they had a great future ahead of them.

'Yet not all of you could keep away, not entirely,' Amy said softly. 'Every fifty years, something draws people to Swallow Woods. It pulls at you, like a magnet. That's why you stayed here rather than go off to London, isn't it? You knew there was a secret here.

Something huge. Something vast. The story of your life. That's what's kept you here, writing about birthday parties and shop openings and exam results. You were waiting for something to happen, something that would explain everything strange and unspoken about the town. Well, it's happening now. I don't know how it ends. I don't know what turns this place from a thriving little market town to a lake and a ghost town. What I do know is that it starts tonight. It starts when you go into Swallow Woods. You're going, Jess. You can go alone and be lost for ever, or I can come with you and maybe – just *maybe* – you'll come out again.'

The jukebox blared out suddenly, the opening bars of 'You Ain't Seen Nothing Yet'. Jess nearly jumped out of her chair.

'Will you let me come with you?' Amy said. 'Or are you going alone?'

Before Jess could answer, Charlie sauntered over.

'This birthday party is obviously going to be the event of the year,' he said, with a curious look at Amy. 'You two have been plotting all night.'

'Unmissable,' Jess said, as cheerfully as could be managed under the circumstances. 'I'll get you an invitation.'

Charlie laughed. 'Well in case I have to be somewhere less thrilling, here's my number.' He passed her a slip of paper. 'Anyone willing to skip drinks to do a report on an eighty-fourth birthday is either mad enough or dedicated enough to be my kind of person. Twins or not. Give me a call, Lois, if the partying doesn't finish you off first.'

He went on his way with a wave and a smile as bright as city lights.

Jess stared at the mobile number scrawled on the paper. This was her chance, at last. She could go home, have a bath, watch *Newsnight* while Lily complained about it being boring, and tomorrow she could call Charlie and maybe get the interview she had always dreamed of…

A pleasant fantasy, one which Jess knew wasn't going to happen. Instead, she would get halfway home, and then she would turn the car round. She would drive back to Long Lane and park somewhere dark and quiet. Then she would climb the fence and cross the field, and she would walk into Swallow Woods. And then?

'Eighty-fourth birthday party?' said Amy.

Jess stuck the piece of paper in a small pouch at the front of her big leather bag.

'Twins, no less,' she said. 'Our cover story,

you strange and alarming woman. Did you really want the paparazzi hanging round while we go into the woods?'

Amy sagged back in her chair in relief. 'Oh, thank goodness!'

'Story of my life, you said. What exactly am I supposed to do? I must be out of my mind, but I'm coming.'

He woke to a splitting headache and the certain knowledge that he was in trouble. It felt like this was not an uncommon occurrence, even if he was fairly sure that he had never surfaced feeling hung over on an alien spaceship before.

Because that was certainly where he was. Even with his eyes still shut, he could tell – from the throb of distant engines pitched for non-human ears, from the stale thickness of air pushed too many times through recycling. Yes, this was an alien spaceship. Interesting. He seemed to know about spaceships.

Then he opened his eyes, and his world became incoherent once again. Because through his blurry vision, it was quite obvious that he was in woodland; woodland in October, when the leaves were mottled green and yellow, suspended between their summer splendour and their fall, waiting for one mighty gust of wind to rip them from the branches. Yes, this looked like woodland – but it didn't *sound* like it, and it didn't *smell* like it…

Too much contradictory information at once. He clamped his eyes shut.

'Where?' he moaned. 'When? And why oh why oh why?'

Somebody moved alongside him. He cracked open an eye. 'Who? Who's there?'

A young woman swam into view. She had a round pretty face and long brown hair. She took hold of his hand.

'It's me, Mr Williams. Emily Bostock. How are you feeling now? You've been away a while!'

She helped him to sit up. Blinking to clear his vision, he had to agree with his semi-conscious self that they were indeed on board some ship, in what seemed to be a small empty hold of some kind. The walls, when he put his hand against them, were metallic, but patterned like a wood in autumn. They were lit from within, and when his hand touched the surface, the light seemed to gather around it. All very puzzling, but it was not his most pressing worry.

'Mr Williams,' he said. 'Um. Who's that?'

The woman who called herself Emily

sat back on her heels and looked at him in consternation.

'Oh goodness me! Can't you remember your name? You're Rory. Rory Williams.'

'Rory' shook his head. Mistake. Black spots appeared alarmingly in front of his eyes, and for one moment he thought his vision was going the same way as his memories.

'I'll have to take your word for that.' He looked at Emily suspiciously. 'Er, I suppose I can trust you, can't I?'

'*What*? You cheeky, bloomin'—!' The young woman slapped his arm, hard. 'If anyone here shouldn't be trusting anyone else, it's me shouldn't be trusting you! My goodness, I'm not sure you've said a straight word to me since we met!'

'All right, all right!' Rory (he'd go with that) pointed at his forehead. 'Head injury! Possibly fatal! Fatal as in fatal death!'

He couldn't, in fact, remember a single thing he had ever said to this woman, chiefly because he couldn't remember ever having met her before, but the feeling of being in trouble with a girl with long hair was vaguely familiar. So was his general sense of bewilderment as to the cause of the girl's fury.

'Look, please, just stop… *beating* me, and

let me think for a minute, will you?' He put his hands to his head. The throb of the engine wasn't helping.

'So you're Emily,' he said at last.

'Well, I told you that!'

'And we're on an alien spaceship.'

She blinked. 'Is that where we are?'

'Er, *look*.' Rory gestured around. 'What else is this going to be?'

'How am I supposed to know? You're the one who knew what was going on!'

'You're the one that ran off!'

'Ooh, so you remember that! You rotten liar! What else do you remember, I wonder?'

'Excuse me! Blow to the head! Fatal injury of fatal death!'

They glared furiously at each other for a few moments, and then Emily began to laugh.

'You look so cross it's comical. Sorry, Mr Williams, but you're about as scary as a rabbit!'

'Right. OK. So we've established that I'm Rory, you're Emily, we're on an alien spaceship, and that I'm a figure of fun. We're definitely getting somewhere.' He sighed. 'But what we're doing here is anyone's guess.'

'You said you were looking for the engine,' Emily said unexpectedly. 'You were going to dismantle it. You said the engine was leaking.'

'I said all that? Doesn't sound like me. Sounds… um, well, competent. What else did I say?'

'Not much. You came into the pub, walked me halfway home, and then told me you had to find a machine in Swallow Woods to take it away. That was about the size of it. Oh, you said you weren't a spy, but I'm starting to think you are. One of ours, though. I bet it's some Hun war machine you're after. And I'll tell you something else for nothing – I wish I'd never laid eyes on you!'

'A spy? That doesn't sound much like me either.' Rory stood up and looked round. There were two exits from the room – one on their left, one on their right – dark archways without doors and not much clue as to what might lie beyond them. 'Right. Er. Which way shall we go?'

'Oh, for heaven's sake! Do you have a coin?'

'What? Oh.' Rory rummaged in his pocket and found a ten pence piece. 'Will that do?'

'That'll do fine. Heads, we go left; tails, we go right.'

Emily flicked the coin into the air and it fell on the ground with a clatter. She stooped to pick it up. 'Heads it is… Here, whose head's that? Is this a foreign coin? You're not a bloomin' Hun after all, are you? That'd be the absolute limit...' She turned the coin over. 'Ten pence. Two-thousand-and-nine. You know, Mr Williams,' she said, as she handed the coin back, 'if I thought about it too much, I could be very scared of you. Nothing queer ever happened to me before I met you. Now look where I am. You could be a villain for all I know – following young women, luring them into the woods. I wish I knew if I could trust you.'

She sounded so woeful that Rory couldn't help but feel a stab of sympathy for her. 'I don't feel like a villain,' he said, 'but then I don't suppose anyone does.' He nodded at the left-hand door. 'Do you like the look of that way?'

'Not much,' Emily admitted.

'Me neither. Let's go the other way.' He put the coin in his pocket, and his fingers brushed against something metal. He pulled out a small triangular object on which green lights were flashing. Something tugged hard at the back of his mind, but when he fumbled around for the memory, all he found was a black hole.

He showed the device to Emily. 'Any idea?'

She shook her head ruefully. 'You never showed me that. Here, what d'you think the buttons do?'

Rory's thumb hesitated over one of them. But you couldn't be too careful.

'Best not,' he said, and shoved the triangulator back into his pocket. 'OK. Right-hand door it is.'

England, now, much closer to closing time

'But we haven't heard a peep out of Rory since we left him in 1917,' Amy told Jess. 'Look, I know it's a lot to take on board all at once, but I've found that if you don't bother worrying about how it can possibly make sense, it suddenly all makes sense. If I'm making any sense.'

They were sitting in Jess's car, which she had parked on Long Lane, near the start of the footpath that led across the fields past Swallow Woods. A century earlier, Rory and Emily had passed this way, before vanishing.

'Oh, I'm following you,' Jess said. 'I'm not sure I like where it's taking me, but I'm following you. Carry on.'

Amy began winding her scarf back round her neck. 'OK, so we waited and we waited. I was supposed to go after Laura into Swallow Woods, but we didn't get the signal from Rory in time. Next thing we knew, Laura was gone. We hopped back to 1917 to take a look, and there was Rory heading into the woods with Emily.' She frowned. 'Oh, yes, very cosy... Anyway, that meant everything was still going to plan. We nipped back to now, and I got ready to follow Vicky Caine. But still no signal from Rory. So we popped forwards fifty years to see if there was anyone else we could follow, and that's when we found out that the woods and the town weren't there! We were both getting a bit panicky now – well, I was – because we knew then that you were the last one, and that if I didn't go with you, we'd have missed our chance, and that whatever is going to happen will happen... Will have happened... Oh, you know what I mean! Don't think about it too hard. Not to mention that poor Rory was nowhere to be found... A perfectly straightforward clean-up job. What a joke! Nothing's ever straightforward with the Doctor.'

'The Doctor. Yeah, I've seen him around,' said Jess. 'You notice new people here. Particularly new people like *that*. Tall, thin, jumps around as if someone's put a hundred-and-fifty volts through him. Oh, and the bow tie, of course. Very dapper. Makes him look like someone senior in *Mad Men*.'

'Dapper?' said Amy in disgust. 'That bow tie is a disgrace— Hey! You know the Doctor?'

'Small town, and my job is to know what's happening in it. I know when people go missing, and I know when strangers pop up from nowhere and start hanging around Swallow Woods. Particularly when one of them wears a bow tie and jumps up and down a lot. You're both a touch cracked, aren't you?'

'Maybe. But that doesn't mean we're not telling you the truth.'

'Hmm. Well, I've been trying to keep tabs on your friend. Not an easy job, given that those occasions when he left town for a few days now turn out to be minor excursions backwards and forwards through time. Still, I've done my best, even if my poor car's racked up the mileage.' She patted the dashboard. 'Could have been worse, I suppose.'

'Oh, so *that's* why it took so long to find you!' Amy rolled her eyes heavenwards. 'While I was dragging around town looking for you, you were busy driving about looking for the Doctor! Well, that's great. That's typical. Anyway, you'd have struggled to find him today—'

'—because he's helping the police with their enquiries.' Jess turned the key in the ignition and the engine and the lights went off. 'Poor Gordon Galloway. I think he may have drawn the short straw. At least you occasionally make sense.' She smiled at Amy through the darkness. 'Told you it was my business to know everything that happens around here.'

'OK, now I'm officially speechless.'

'Thank goodness for that… Are you ready for our excellent adventure, Amy? I think it's about due to start.'

'Always ready,' said Amy, and grinned.

They left the car, crossed the lane, and climbed over the fence. As they walked across the field, Jess said, 'Don't you get scared, Amy?'

'Scared? Of course. But even when things are scary, they're still amazing.'

'I didn't mean that so much as… Tinkering with time. Don't you worry you'll get something wrong? Break things somehow so that they can't be put right?'

'You can't think that way,' Amy said. 'You'd be paralysed if you did. If I've learned anything from the Doctor, it's that it's always better to act. It's always better to do *something*. OK, and then it's true that you have to accept the consequences. But if you think about it, nobody's guaranteed a happy ending, are they? Not in the great scheme of things. And you never know in advance what ending is best.'

'Not much different from real life, then?'

'Not really, no. Sometimes the heebie-jeebies

are worse.'

The trees were now very close. 'I think I understand where you're coming from,' Jess said, feeling some heebie-jeebies of her own.

'Ready?'

'Ready.'

The two young women clasped hands, and together walked into Swallow Woods.

At once, the light changed. They were no longer walking at night through a wood on the cusp of winter. Here, now – wherever and whenever this was – it was daytime, and it was summer.

'Oh,' Jess whispered.

'OK,' said Amy briskly. 'Don't worry. This'll be one of those warp thingies the Doctor was talking about. It's a perfectly normal side effect of this particular kind of interstellar drive. We'll soon get used to it.'

'Amy, your voice is shaking.'

'Is it? Well, the Doctor said that disorientation was…'

'Perfectly normal?' Jess brushed her hand through the thick green leaves of the nearest tree sending golden trails of pollen drifting down. 'So as soon as time starts progressing in a linear fashion, and the paths start going where I expect them to go – that's when I should start worrying?'

'That's when you should start worrying,' Amy confirmed. They looked at each other and burst out laughing. 'It's amazing, though, isn't it?' Amy said. 'Like stepping through a portal and coming out on another world.' She frowned. 'I assume that's not actually happened.'

'Would it matter if we had?' Jess said. She felt light-headed; she wasn't sure if it was excitement or shock or fear.

'Well, the TARDIS can travel in space too, so the Doctor could still come and find us – provided the police ever release him. But I do prefer having at least a rough idea of what's happening. You know, minor details, like where I am and when I am.'

They walked on. The woods hummed with life – the sudden sweet chirping of birds; the dry rustle of grass and the crisp crack of wood. The light through the leaves was soft and shimmering.

'I like it here,' Jess said. 'It's as if the birds and the animals have been left to get on with things. There's nobody to hunt them, or disturb them, or harm them. This must be what the world was like before people.' She frowned. 'Although, given what you said about time pockets, this could very well be the world before people. Do you have any idea where we're supposed to be going?'

'Further into the woods,' Amy said. 'Whichever way that is. I'm guessing we'll know when we get near to the ship. We can hear it already, I think. That throbbing sound?'

'Yes, of course, I guess I thought that was the motorway. You know how traffic sounds from a distance. But this is different.'

'Less swooshy?' Amy suggested.

'Less swooshy,' Jess agreed. 'Steadier, more constant. OK, let's follow that.'

They went in single file through the trees. The ground became rough, knotted and gnarled with sudden tree roots or unexpected branches, and they made slow progress. After a little while, the trees quietly parted, and Amy and Jess came into an empty glade.

Here, it was winter. The trees were bare and black, and the air damp with thin grey fog and the moist smell of mulching leaves. The women walked together around the perimeter of the clearing. The barren arms of the trees locked together to form great archways. The mist clung to the boles of the trees, curling around them, so that Amy and Jess could only glimpse the start of the bleak narrow pathways that faded into the darkness.

'Do you know what place this reminds me of?' Jess spoke in a respectful whisper. 'The parish church in the village. St Jude's. But a ruin. It's like we're in a ruined church.'

'St Jude?' Amy whispered back. 'That's the patron saint of lost causes. Your town is *creepy*.'

She walked to the centre of the clearing, where a deep pool of water lay. She dipped her fingertips into the dark liquid and tasted it. Brackish and bitterly cold. Something by the pool's edge caught her eye and Amy reached over to pick it up. It was a brooch of some kind, jet black, in the shape of a butterfly, scuffed and scarred, as if it had been here for ever. She showed it to Jess.

'Pretty,' she said. 'I don't recognise it though.'

'Me neither.' Amy pinned the brooch to her jacket. She imagined it as a gift from someone to his beloved. Now it was lost, for good. Suddenly Amy felt very sad. She longed to see Rory again; hold his hand, joke with him, kiss him, know that he was safe. Where could he be? Was he lost for good? Amy shut her eyes and touched the tiny jet object, as if it could somehow link her to Rory, through time. She could almost imagine that he was here, now, standing beside her; she could almost feel his breath upon the back of her neck…

'Who's there?' Jess cried out.

Amy's eyes shot open. Spinning round, she saw a figure dash across the glade towards a gap between the thickly woven trees. Both women moved quickly, too quickly for their prey. They got to the gap first, blocking the escape route. Jess grabbed one arm, Amy the other.

'Oh no you don't!' said Amy, as they turned the figure round to face them. 'Come on, let's take a look at you!'

Jess gasped, recognising her immediately. Amy recognised her too. So would anyone in the country. Her face had been appearing almost non-stop on television and the front pages of the papers for the last four days.

'My watch,' Vicky Caine whispered. 'My watch stopped.'

'A ship,' Rory mused out loud, as he and Emily walked slowly along the dim corridor. 'But is it in flight? Could we be heading somewhere? And why haven't we seen any crew? Where are they?'

'You said the machine was dead, remember?' Emily ran her finger along the wall, from which a gentle yellowish glow was emanating. The light responded to her touch, as it had to Rory's palm in the hold earlier, thickening around her fingertip as she drew it along. 'I feel like I'm still in the woods. In October. But the air's stale. I can tell we're not really outside.'

'A ship like this would have to be tightly sealed if it was going to be able to move about in space,' Rory said.

'I know that,' Emily said. 'Like something in a story by Mr Wells. Me and Sam used to read him to each other.'

'Sam?' Rory looked around, bewildered. 'Who's Sam? Is there someone else here? Why haven't you mentioned him before? Emily, you've got to tell me everything, you don't know what's important!'

'Oh, shut up,' said Emily miserably. 'Sam? Where do you think he is? Sam's dead.'

'Dead?' Desperately, Rory searched through his memories, but he only found empty spaces where this knowledge should have been. Could he forget someone's death? What else had he forgotten? Who else had he forgotten? 'When? What happened?'

'More than a year ago, you fool! In the War. We should have been married by now. But Sammy's dead and I've got myself lost in the woods...' Emily stopped walking. She turned her back to Rory, but he could tell from her shoulders that she was crying. Awkwardly, he placed his hand against her back and, when she didn't shake it off, he put his arm around her with more confidence, sure that this was the right thing to do.

She wept for a little while into his shoulder, not noisily but very quietly, like this was something she had done a lot in private. As Rory held her, he felt the faintest echo of a memory – of someone he loved very much, that he would give eternity to be with – but before he could grab hold, the memory drifted sadly away like leaves in autumn. He hugged Emily even more.

'Shush,' he said. 'I'm sorry. It'll be OK. It'll be OK again, one day.'

Eventually, Emily stopped crying. They hugged each other again for good measure. 'Pals?' said Emily.

'Pals,' said Rory.

Emily dried her face and gave a rueful laugh. 'Bet I look a right old mess,' she said. 'Stupid bloomin' War. Ruins everything, don't it? You can't get a drink after half past nine, and you can't get married to your sweetheart.' She found a hankie in her pocket and blew her nose. 'And there's that wretched humming again. I'll

tell you something for nothing, Mr Williams –
I know you said you were here to take away
the engine because it was dead. But I wonder
if you were right about that. Because this place
doesn't seem the least bit dead to me. The lights,
the noise. It looks to me like it's still in working
order. Asleep, maybe, but not dead. Alive.'

England, now, shortly before one in the morning

Galloway burst through the door of the
interview room as if he were a thunderstorm
howling through.

He found his chief suspect standing right up
by the window, one cheek pressed against the
dark glass, a look of deep concentration on his
jumbled-up face. Since their last conversation,
the young man had apparently fixed the blind,
which was raised up out of the way to allow
him to get as close to the window as possible.
The clock had not fared so well. It had been
dismantled, and now lay in pieces on the table.

'How?' Galloway shouted. 'How did you
know?'

The chief suspect flapped his hand. 'Ssh! I'm
trying to listen!'

'*Listen*? Now look here, sonny, I've just about
had enough of you!'

'Sir!' Porter grabbed Galloway's arm, holding him back.

Galloway got himself back under control. Pressing his hands flat against the table top, he said, in a much quieter voice, 'How did you know that Jess Ashcroft was going to go missing? We've found her car, up by the woods. Do you have an accomplice? Is it the red-headed girl? You've been seen in the company of a red-headed girl, so was Jess. Is she your accomplice? Or is she another victim?'

The young man looked round. He raised one finger, like he was about to issue a ticking-off. 'You,' he said, 'are a very noisy man. Now listen!'

'I'm trying to talk to you!'

'And I'm trying to listen! Shush!'

'But—'

'Lips! Sealed! Now!'

'Sir,' Porter said quietly, 'it can't do any harm.'

The three of them stood and listened, but all Galloway could hear was the steady pitter-patter of rain against the window. He felt like a fool. 'There's nothing,' he said, impatiently. 'Nothing at all.'

'You can't hear it?' The young man frowned and pressed his ear back against the window. 'I can't be the only one who can hear it…'

Porter, unexpectedly, said, 'I can.'

The young man swung round to face her. He stared at her as if noticing her properly for the first time. 'Yes! *You*! You can hear it!'

He was becoming extremely excited. Carefully, Galloway put himself between the suspect and Porter.

'You've lived here your whole life, haven't you?' the young man said. 'Not him. Not with that accent, as Pond-like as Pond herself. But *you*,' he pointed both his forefingers at Porter. 'Oh I could kiss you!' He pulled back. 'I won't, though, that would be weird… But you can hear it too! I'm not hearing things! Or, rather, I *am* hearing things, but not in the way that leads to awkward conversations, more awkward than usual… You! Yes! You've heard it your whole life, haven't you? And I *missed* it!'

He swung back to face the window. He banged his forehead against it and the blind came crashing down on top of his head. Now he had to struggle to disentangle himself, talking all the while.

'Oh, there's too much noise in this day and age! With your clocks and your 24-hour rolling news and your non-stop reality shows and your CB radio transmissions…'

He managed to get out from under the blind, which slumped back glumly into its former diagonal position.

Porter and Galloway exchanged a look. *CB radio…?*

'All that blathering and chattering and texting and phoning in – no wonder I could hardly hear anything! But it's there, isn't it? Oh yes, it's there. The propulsion unit, the engine, the nice hot cup of tea. Not dead. Not dead at all. Still running. All I had to do was *listen*!'

'You've stopped making sense,' said Porter. 'What's not dead? What's still running?'

As she repeated his words, the young man stopped still and stared at her as if a terrible realisation had struck him. The effect was rather like lightning hitting a gangly and over-excited telegraph pole.

'Oh,' he said, 'but if it's still running, then that changes things. Because it couldn't run indefinitely. Not for thousands of years, anyway. It would need maintenance… And maintenance means someone… someone's there… I've let them go off with those ridiculous triangular things, and the ship hasn't been abandoned at all! There's somebody there!'

'You mean in Swallow Woods?' said Porter. 'Who?' she urged. 'Who's there?'

'Well, who else would it be? The pilot, of course. The ship hasn't been abandoned! The pilot's still here!'

Chapter
9

People. Holding her down, stopping her getting away. Vicky struggled, but their arms were around her, unyielding, like a nightmare tangle of tree branches pressing, scratching, trapping her. She looked round desperately for a place to hide, but the woods were wintry and offered no cover. She struggled, futilely, and then realised that her captors were talking to her, shushing her, trying to calm her, saying her name.

'Vicky, it's OK.' A Scottish accent. 'Vicky, we won't hurt you. You're safe.'

'My watch,' she said, trying to make them understand. It was so important that they understood; that they knew about everything that was happening here. Perhaps if they understood, they could explain it to her. 'My watch stopped!'

'We know,' said another voice; someone local. 'Don't worry, sweetheart. Are you OK?'

'No!' Vicky said, and then burst into tears. 'My mum's going to kill me!'

One of them let go of her; the other person's hold relaxed, turning into an embrace. Vicky felt herself rocked gently to and fro. 'No she won't,' said the local one, a soft reassuring breath in her ear. 'She's going to be thrilled to see you.'

'Bet you get a new watch out of it,' said the other. 'At the very least.'

Vicky couldn't help but laugh, even through her tears. 'I'll be choosing my own watches in future, thanks!'

She received another hug for that.

'Good on you, kiddo,' said the Scottish voice. 'I'm Amy, by the way. And this is Jess.'

Rubbing her eyes, Vicky took a proper look at her erstwhile captors. Two young women: one very tall and with amazing long red hair; the other shorter and with serious glasses that Vicky bet could make her look impressively stern if she put her mind to it. But she was the one with her arms round Vicky, the one who had spoken so softly. They both wore expressions of real concern. Vicky started to feel better.

They sat her down under one of the trees.

Amy went to get her a drink of water, and then knelt down in front of her. Jess kept tight hold of her hand.

'OK,' Amy said. 'Why don't you tell us what happened. And don't worry if it sounds like rubbish. We'll believe you.'

Again Vicky showed them her watch. It still showed five to ten, as it had been for, for... however long she had been wandering around here – hours, days, weeks – she had no idea now. 'It was like it was stuck. I couldn't get it to start again!'

Jess looked down at her own watch, then shook it, and lifted it up to her ear. 'Snap,' she said. 'Go on.'

'So I missed the last bus. Decided to walk—I know! I know!' she said, seeing them both roll their eyes. 'I should have just asked for a lift! But it was getting late, and I didn't want to bother Frank and Carole. I couldn't get a signal on my phone... I took a shortcut – should have been fine, nobody comes this way... And then I fell and rolled down the hill, and the clouds came out and I couldn't see the lights any more... Next thing I knew I was under the trees! It was so dark. I could hardly see my hand in front of me. I kept walking. The woods aren't that big, are they? I had to reach the edge at some point.

I could hear cars on the motorway, so I thought I'd better walk in that direction.'

Amy and Jess exchanged a look. 'I'm guessing the edge of the woods never turned up,' Amy said.

'No. Sometimes the sound got louder and sometimes it went away. And I never got any closer...'

Jess squeezed her shoulder. 'What happened next?'

Vicky gestured round the glade. 'I got here... It was exactly like it is now. Winter. The trees were bare and dead. I realised that it was getting light, and I knew that was my best chance of getting out, so I didn't stop. I left that way.' She pointed to one of the arches formed by the trees, over to their right. 'At least, I think it was that way. I walked along the path for a while, and I saw some daylight, and I got really excited – but when I went towards it, I ended up back here.' She took a deep breath. 'This next bit's weird, really weird—'

'Trust me,' Amy said, 'there's nothing you can say that will sound weird to me.'

Vicky eyed her doubtfully, but carried on. 'I went another way and the same thing happened. I came back here. Then I started marking the paths with pine cones, so I'd know I wasn't going the same way twice. Eventually I'd tried them all – I *know* I had! Every single path had a pine cone next to it.' Her voice started getting louder. 'But how could that happen? One of them *had* to be the path that brought me here, didn't it? How could that one lead me back, same as the rest? I don't understand it!'

'Shush, it's all OK,' said Jess. 'We're here now. What happened next?'

'By this time I was really tired and it was starting to get dark again. I sat down for a while, and I fell asleep. When I woke up…' She shook her head again. 'You're never going to believe this…'

'Want to bet?' Amy said. 'Remember – weird is fine.'

'Well… when I woke up, it was spring.'

Amy smiled at her. Jess just blinked.

'OK, that is fairly weird,' Amy agreed. 'But, yes, that's the time pockets. It makes perfect sense.'

'It does *feel* weird, though,' Jess said.

'I thought you'd tell me I was being stupid,' Vicky said in relief. 'Or that I must have still been asleep. But I wasn't. I was definitely awake. I woke up and it was spring. The leaves were green and the birds were singing, and everything smelt of rain and growing. I know

121

I can't have been asleep because I got up and went to the pool for a drink of water. I can't have dreamed that, can I? Do you think I must have dreamed it?'

'Neither of us think you were dreaming, Vicky,' Jess said, quietly. She rubbed the girl's arm, partly for warmth, partly for comfort. 'Carry on.'

'OK... So I was sitting there drinking from the pool, and then... well, what happened next was summer. It came all in a rush. I couldn't believe what I was seeing... The buds on the trees sprouted and popped open, the leaves unfurled, and then the blossom appeared and grew and then fell – it was like one of those nature films where they speed everything up... I don't know how long it took, my watch is stuck... It got so warm I had to take my coat off. And the noise, what I thought had been the motorway, that got steadily louder. I had to put my fingers in my ears. I walked around the clearing, trying to work out where it was coming from, but it seemed to be everywhere all at once. And then...'

She stopped and took a very deep breath. She was staring over at one of the archways formed by two trees. 'There,' she said, pointing at the archway, 'There was someone there.'

'*Laura*?' mouthed Jess to Amy, over Vicky's head. To Vicky, she said, 'Can you describe who it was?'

'There's another girl missing in Swallow Woods,' Amy explained. 'Do you think it could have been her? She's a little taller than Jess, but not as tall as me; younger than us but a couple of years older than you. She was wearing a bright red coat and she's got short black hair—'

Vicky shook her head quickly. 'No, no – this was someone with reddish, brownish hair. And I think it was a he, not a she. I'm pretty sure of that.'

Amy's stomach twisted. Could it have been Rory?

'OK,' she said, trying to sound calm so that she didn't frighten Vicky, 'did this person talk to you? Did they say or do anything at all?' She would know at once if it was Rory, probably from the gabbling.

But Vicky had closed her eyes, and had started to tremble. Clearly the memory of this person frightened her in some way – but the only person Rory had a chance of frightening was himself.

'He didn't say anything,' Vicky said. 'He stood under one of the tree arches and he beckoned to me to follow. Well, that wasn't going to happen, not in a million years!'

'Good for you,' said Jess.

'It was a close thing, though. I don't know what he was doing, but I felt like I had to follow him. The noise had got really loud now, maybe that was something to do with it, because it was like a magnet was pulling at me, trying to make me go through one of the arches. I wasn't going to follow a stranger anywhere, but I felt like I should run away – away through one of the other arches. But I didn't fancy that much, either. So I climbed a tree and I put my headphones on and I sang along—'

'Oh, good thinking!' Amy said.

'—and eventually the leaves started going red and gold, and then it was winter again. But that was even worse in a way. Because everything was dead, and there weren't any birds. I couldn't even hear the throbbing noise. There was nothing. I just wanted to go home!' She started to cry. 'I really, really want to go home! Mum's going to kill me—'

'No. Really, that isn't going to happen,' Jess promised.

'You're in luck, kiddo,' Amy said. 'Everyone's going to be over the moon to see you. But next time – stick to the path. Better still, call a taxi or stay the night, OK?'

As Jess explained to Vicky how she and Amy had got there, Amy walked slowly around the clearing, one hand brushing along the circle of trees. At each gap between them, she paused to peer through, trying to decide which way would be best. The mist had begun to dissipate, but each of the paths leading out from the clearing rose slightly and then fell away, making it difficult to see what lay beyond. Vicky may have been mistaken, too tired and too distressed to see that she was following the same paths over and over – but what if she was right? What if by some unlucky concatenation of space-time pockets, all these paths did come back here? They could soon exhaust themselves, walking round and round in circles, and that wouldn't leave them in a fit state to deal with whoever it was that Vicky had seen. Perhaps it was better simply to stay here in the clearing. At some point the Doctor was bound to turn up…

Based on previous experience, however, Amy knew that could take anything up to twelve years. Besides – sitting around and waiting? Hardly her style. The Doctor didn't travel with people who sat around waiting for him to come and save them, did he? He travelled with people who made a choice about what to do, then went off and did it. Didn't he?

And what would happen to the town while she was sitting twiddling her thumbs? She couldn't rely on the Doctor being free in time – which put him in danger too. She couldn't just push the button on the triangulator. She had to get to the ship first, or the TARDIS would be lost in the woods too. And of course, there would be no help from Rory – wherever he was, he was clearly having trouble of his own. Amy was going to have to deal with her own problems and (she glanced over at Vicky and Jess) other responsibilities. Things weren't too bad, though. There was no sign, for example, of anything happening that might cause a devastating flood. On the other hand, what if whatever she decided to do next *was* the cause...?

Amy shook her herself. You couldn't think that way. You'd end up sitting in a tree watching the water lap around your ankles if you thought that way. You had to act.

'Right,' she said, turning round to face the others. 'I'm not thrilled with any of our options right now, but I think probably the worst one is to sit here and wait for the woods to flood. Agreed?'

'Agreed,' Jess said.

'Flood?' Vicky sounded shaky again.

'Yeah. Best not to worry about that right now.'

Vicky looked decidedly un-reassured. 'But which way will we go?' she said. 'I told you – I've tried all the paths. They all come back here.'

'We'll try again,' said Amy, firmly. 'There are three of us now – three sets of eyes, three sets of ears. We're much more likely to spot something that will give us a clue as to how to get out of here.'

'We could split up,' Jess said. 'You take one exit, and I take the next one along with Vicky?'

'Splitting up,' said Amy, 'is always a terrible option. Don't you watch TV?'

'Fair point,' said Jess. 'OK, I guess it's a kind of logic puzzle. If we're going to solve it, we're going to have to work out exactly what sort of puzzle it is, gather as much data as we can, and just do some serious thinking.'

'Uh. I was going to toss a coin,' said Amy.

Vicky was starting to doubt the suitability of her rescuers for the task. 'Whatever we do,' she said urgently, 'I think we need to do it soon. Look, look at the trees. It's starting again…'

She was right. In the short time that Amy had spent walking round, the trees had begun to bud. Even as she watched, new leaves began to emerge. Soon the whole glade was rustling with growth, and the damp, lonely smell of winter was chased away by something warmer and greener.

Jess stood up and looked around in delight. 'It's amazing! I should be afraid, I know, but it's so wonderful!' She gasped and pointed across the glade. 'Oh, look! Look! Over there! A fox!'

There it sat, beneath one of the great arches of trees, its head cocked to one side, watching them.

'It's beautiful!' Jess said, and Amy had to agree. A sudden plash of sunlight through the quickening leaves caught upon its red fur, lighting up the points like flames licking upwards. Its bib was white and its eyes orange. Even though Amy knew it was a mistake to project human emotion onto animals, she thought the eyes looked sad and aged. Perhaps it was the tilt of the creature's head, and the greying flecks of fur above its eyes. Even without imagining things, this was certainly an old animal.

The fox rose slowly to its feet, still watching them. It lifted its front right paw, as if it was about to trot away. Then it stepped onto its hind legs and began to change shape.

'OK,' Amy said. 'This is a new one…'

'What?' said Jess. 'What, what, *what*?'

The transformation took about a minute, by which time the fox was the size and the shape of a human, perhaps somewhat slighter than the average man. The face remained distinctly vulpine – long-muzzled, black ears perched upright at the top of its head, the hair thicker than human hair, more pelt-like, and reddish. No, this was definitely not Rory – unless Rory had forgotten to mention something, and Rory wouldn't dare.

'You didn't mention he was a fox,' Jess remarked to Vicky.

'That's because this bit didn't happen!'

As they watched, the fox-man turned away as if to go. He looked back over his shoulder, and then beckoned to them to follow him along the path.

'Amy,' Jess said, 'not to put you on the spot, but I think you might have slightly more experience with this kind of thing than either me or Vicky. Ought we to go with it?'

'No!' said Vicky quickly.

'Or should we keep well away?'

All the time the transformation had been happening, Amy had been thinking furiously. There was no way of knowing whether this was a good fox-guy or a bad fox-guy, or something in between. But here at least was a face to all the mystery surrounding Swallow Woods. Time pockets, spatial warps, swiftly changing seasons – there was nothing to latch onto there. But here, for the first time, was someone she could reason with.

Besides, perhaps it might be satisfied with one of them.

'OK,' Amy said. 'First of all, I want you to not argue with me, and I want you to listen.'

'You're about to say something I won't like, right?' Jess said.

'Yes, and you're still not to argue. I want you to go, Jess, and I want you to take Vicky with you—I said don't argue! I'm going to follow Fantastic Mr Fox, and I want you two to go in the opposite direction.'

'Amy,' Jess said quickly, 'that's a terrible idea! What if you're lost for good? I don't know enough about what's going on to be able to help—'

'Oh, who ever knows enough!' cried Amy. A leaf above her turned yellow, crisped, and fell to the ground. The man-fox, whatever he called himself, began to back up the path. He was still beckoning to them, but soon he would be out of sight.

Amy rolled her triangulator around in her

fingers. 'Here's what I'm thinking. If I don't go now, we'll only end up sitting around waiting here till summer comes again and this place reactivates. Who knows what will happen in the meantime?'

'Amy, maybe it's you going with this beastie that causes the whole thing—!'

'That's a chance we're going to have to take.' Amy lifted her hand to acknowledge the creature, and took a step towards it. 'Jess, I'm going now. Take Vicky and leave here. If you get through – try to reach the Doctor. Tell him I've still got the triangulator—'

'The *what*-you-later?'

'Oh, just say the chocolate device! He'll know what I mean!'

Autumn was coming fast. All around, the clearing was changing colour, the leaf-fall getting thicker. Amy broke into a run. At the entry to the arch, she paused, and pointed across the clearing. 'Go now!' she shouted to Jess and Vicky. 'Go that way! It's worth a try! Go on! And good luck!'

'Wait!' shouted Jess. 'You said we shouldn't split up!'

'I was wrong! Who'd have guessed! Go *now*!'

Amy knew she couldn't risk waiting any

longer. She ducked beneath the archway of trees, and followed the fox – wherever he was leading her. Behind her, she could still hear Jess, calling to her forlornly.

'Amy! Did you really say the *chocolate* device?'

Alive. Now Emily had said it, Rory found it hard not to agree. The lights from the walls, shifting and shimmering, were like sunlight passing through leaves, as if the decorators had tried their best to emulate a forest. The effect was disorientating, like travelling on a train and watching the scenery so intently you started to think that you were motionless and the world was moving at high speed.

When, wondered the-man-who-was-calling-himself-Rory, had he travelled on a train? Where to? Where from? Would he start to remember? Or was the story of his life gone for good?

'I think we're arriving somewhere,' Emily said, softly. She pointed up ahead, where the corridor ended in an archway. The metal panels on either side were etched with long lines, like the branches of a tree. Rory ran his fingertip along one of them, and a trail of light followed his touch.

'I wonder why the design seems so familiar,'

he said.

'Looks like the arches in the parish church,' Emily said. 'Not to mention the trees we came under before we turned up here. You don't remember, do you?'

Rory shook his head. They walked through the doorway into the room beyond. The effect was like entering a woodland glade – only one made from metals and plastics. The walls loomed around, like heavy old grey trees, and in the centre of the room was a large flat circular console, its surface dark and empty like a pool in winter. Steps led down to it from where they stood, and a second set of steps led up to another doorway opposite.

'Where do you think we are?' Emily said.

Rory shrugged. 'Control room of some sort?'

'I wish I knew how you were so sure of these things!'

'Me too… But it seems obvious.'

'Anyone would think you'd been on a – what did you call it?'

'Spaceship.'

'One of them. Anyone would think you'd been on one before.'

Perhaps he had. Before or after he'd been on a train. Rory walked slowly down the steps and stood in front of the console. 'Hello!' he said, and then: 'Computer!'

Nothing happened. Emily, standing next to him, waved her hand at the surface of the console. It sprang to life: writing and images started scrolling past at a great rate, like ripples on water, and a control panel of virtual buttons appeared, following Emily's hand around as she moved it.

'How did you know to do that?' said Rory.

'Well, if they're alien, they might not know English. Waving seemed friendly. Here, what do you think all this is saying?'

'Greek to me...'

'What, *actual* Greek?'

'Well, the alien equivalent of Greek. If aliens have an equivalent of Greek—'

'You do go on, you know. What do you think would happen if I press this red button here?'

Rory grabbed her hand. 'Emily! You never, ever press red buttons!'

'All right.' She snaked her other hand past him and thumped her thumb against the screen. 'I'll try the green one instead.'

Rory threw his arms over his head and dived to the ground.

Emily chuckled. 'You're such an easy target! Come and have a look, this is interesting.'

Gathering up what was left of his dignity, Rory stood up. On the screen, the images and the weird text were rushing past. With some experimentation, Emily found she could slow the pace down; some further tests let them stop and start the flow, but they could not make any sense of the actual words. The pictures, they both noticed, were all of humans.

'Maybe they were the crew,' said Rory.

'But you said this was an alien spaceship?'

'Perhaps I was wrong. Perhaps it's human after all, but from the future.'

'Still full of surprises, aren't you? Look, though, look at the clothes. That dress looks like something my old granny would have worn. And those are Roman!'

Rory, looking at the image, felt himself blush hotly, although he couldn't for the life of him say why.

'They look to me like pictures from the past, not the future,' Emily said. 'Like a history book—Here, I know that one! Go back, go back!'

Rory skimmed back until she told him to stop again.

'That's it!' she said. 'I know him! That's Harry, Harry Thompson! Oh, you won't remember, will you? He's the lad that went missing six weeks ago. We thought he'd run off rather than get called up. And these little pictures – that's his mam and dad, and his three sisters. Their farm backs onto our bottom field. I know them like I know my own family. What are all their pictures doing here, I wonder?'

Rory started scrolling through again, more and more quickly. Was his picture here too? If it was, perhaps they could work out what the text said, work out who he was and where he had come from…

'Slow down, Mr Williams, we might miss something!'

'Emily, I'm trying to see if I'm here—'

'I know that, love, but you're going much too quick.' She rested her hand gently on his, moving it away and stopping the images flooding past. 'Now slow down and let's take a proper look through.'

Slowly, they pored through the pictures. Rory lost count somewhere in the hundred-and-thirties, and he had not even been counting the smaller pictures. There was no sign of a picture of him.

'Less like a history book and more like a catalogue,' he muttered, swiping his hand across the screen so that yet another picture came past. This one looked like a mediaeval peasant.

'Alien abduction... But why on earth would I think that? What is wrong with my *head*? Why won't it sort itself *out*?' Frustrated, he banged the flat of his hand against the console. It made a *thumping* noise. The mottled light from the walls dimmed. Rory looked round anxiously. 'Did I do that?'

'How on earth would I know?' Emily hit the side of the console too, and the light came slowly back to the same level as before. 'Looks like it!'

They both laughed nervously, guiltily, like children who were getting away with some mischief. They stopped laughing when they heard footsteps, coming slowly and heavily along the corridor towards them.

'Oh, Mr Williams,' Emily whispered, her eyes bright with fear, 'what are we going to do?'

Rory didn't stop to think. Summoning up some knowledge from deep, deep within his mind, he grabbed Emily's hand and pulled her towards the doorway opposite. 'What else? Run!'

Tripping over roots, pushing away branches, Amy followed the were-fox through a dark tunnel of trees. He trotted along at a quick pace, every so often turning to check that she was still there, and waving his hand to hurry her. Sometimes he smiled – at least, Amy thought it was a smile. His lips parted to show small, sharp, white teeth. She wasn't sure whether to be alarmed or encouraged.

The path rose again, and the fox-man dipped out of view.

'Oh no, you don't…' Amy ran the last few metres to catch up. The trees were thinning around her, and at last came to an end. With relief, she stepped out into sunshine.

Amy gasped. Ahead of her lay a fantastic landscape. She was standing looking down into a lush green valley set amongst rolling hills, with a swift silver river running through its heart. In the middle distance stood a tall dark turreted building, which looked exactly how a castle would look if built by alien foxes. Amy felt as if she had walked into *Beauty and the Beast*, or a child's picture book of fairy tales in which all the buildings and people were in silhouette.

The fox-man was standing a few yards ahead of her, on the path leading down to the valley. He gave her another sharp white smile.

'OK,' Amy said. 'I'm impressed. Even knowing there are all kinds of spatial wotsits going on around here, I'm still impressed. I'm also tired, so if that's where we're going, I'll need a sit down first.'

The man-fox laughed: a sound somewhere between a rasp and a cough. Not an encouraging noise at all.

'Don't do that again,' said Amy. 'Please. Unless this is the moment where you turn out to be on the dangerous side of scary. In which case – laugh's perfect.'

'Don't be afraid,' said the were-fox. After the laugh, his voice turned out to be surprisingly pleasant, deep and rich, charming, but rather frightening. 'And don't worry about walking, you won't have to.'

Lifting his hand, he waved it in front of him, and the distance between them and the valley collapsed. Now they were standing outside the huge wooden gate of the castle.

'Nice trick,' Amy said gamely. 'All your public transport problems solved. You should speak to the government.'

He waved his hand again, and now they were standing in a broad stone courtyard.

'Lady,' he called out, his deep voice resounding off the stone walls like a great bell. 'I've returned, but only one of them came with me.'

Amy looked around to see who he was addressing. One of the wooden doors around the courtyard opened, and an elderly woman emerged. She was white-haired, but walked quickly towards them. When she reached the fox-man, he bowed with a great show of gallantry, and clasped her hand. Then the old woman turned to Amy.

'Welcome,' she said. She threw her arms around Amy and hugged her with surprising strength. 'Oh, it's been so long since I've seen another human, never mind spoken to one! I'm so glad to see you!'

'OK...' said Amy. 'Um, thanks?'

The old woman released Amy from the embrace, and took hold of both her hands. 'Tell me your name,' she urged.

'Amy. Amy Pond.'

'Amy. Welcome to our kingdom, Amy. I'm Laura Brown.'

The fox-man smiled sharply.

'You know,' said Amy, 'I had a feeling you were going to say that.'

The rain was coming down more heavily, and the wind was picking up, but the police search was finally getting organised at the edge of Swallow Woods. The place where Jess had parked her car, several hours earlier, was cordoned off. Lighting scaffolds were going up; and the distinctive blue and white tape was spreading out across the field which Jess and Amy (and, once upon a time, Rory and Emily) had walked across to enter Swallow Woods.

Galloway watched all this progress with a steadily growing sense of relief. At last, this investigation was properly under way. The quiet country lane, along which he had driven many times in the last eighteen months, was the busiest he had ever seen it. It had not escaped his notice, however, that almost all the officers here were from outside of town. Somehow, the local police had found themselves jobs back at the station – Porter included.

The big lights were ready. Galloway gave the nod, and the field was bathed in their harsh white glare. He climbed over the fence, and stood for a while looking at the woods.

Gathered in the hollow, the trees were dark and impenetrable. They seemed almost to suck in the light. The rain was turning the ground beneath Galloway's feet to mud. He took a few squelching steps forward. Something was moving near the tree-line. An animal? Galloway screwed up his eyes.

Two small figures were moving across the

field towards him. Their progress was slow and unsteady; one of them was leaning on the other, half-carried, half-dragged. They looked like battlefield survivors, pulling themselves bit by bit out of no-man's land. As they came closer, Galloway recognised them. He had been thinking of nothing else for days now.

Galloway broke into a sprint, reaching them before anyone else. He threw his arms around Vicky Caine, and then knelt down before her.

'Oh thank God,' he whispered, brushing a wet lock of hair away from her scratched and dirty face, only realising as he spoke that he had seriously begun to doubt his ability to find them. 'Thank God!'

Jess Ashcroft put her hand on his shoulder. It felt oddly as if she was the one taking care of him.

'So you're all here... Good, good, that's something of a relief, I can tell you.' The harsh searchlights made her look pale and exhausted. 'How long have I been gone? Quickly, Inspector!'

'What?' Her question made no sense. 'Four hours, maybe five?'

She gasped. 'Is that all?'

A couple of paramedics arrived. They covered both girls up, and tried to hurry them towards an ambulance. Vicky was taken off, but Jess wouldn't budge. Grabbing hold of Galloway's arm, she said, 'I need you to do something for me and I need you not to ask any questions. The man you have in custody. You've got to get him here as quickly as possible.'

'*What?*'

'The storm's coming, Mr Galloway. We can't stop it now. Only the Doctor can do that. If we're not too late already.'

Galloway wasn't sure whether she was serious, or just plain mad.

'But we should be OK,' Jess said firmly. 'Amy's still got her chocolate device.'

Chapter
10

Rory and Emily had run out of places to hide. The ship turned out to contain no more than a few empty rooms similar to the one where Rory had woken up, and the passages all led back to the spherical room containing the circular console.

As they arrived there for a third time, Emily started to sound a little desperate. 'We're not going to get away, are we? There's nowhere to hide!'

'Not looking good, is it?'

They ran down the steps and around the back of the console. Rory's thinking was that – perhaps – it was special space plastic and it would act as some sort of barrier between them and whatever was coming. OK. Not very likely.

But possible. There was another door behind them, through which they could run (again) if the need arose, so they wouldn't be completely trapped, even if, in the end, they'd probably just end up back here (again). He looked around for something he could pick up and brandish, but everything was fixed down and, anyway, he wasn't sure how convincing he would look.

The footsteps clanged steadily upon the metal grating. At the doorway, however, they stopped. Rory peered over the console, but the hollow of the room was too low down for him to be able to see out.

'We don't mean you any harm,' he shouted up at their pursuer. 'We hope that's the same for you. Can't we talk?'

'*Talk…*' It was a young man's voice. '*Talk…*'

'OK,' Rory whispered to Emily, 'so whatever it is, at least it's got a throat.'

'Ooh, that doesn't make me feel better!'

'Sorry! Yes! What I meant was that makes it similar to – and therefore less immediately terrifying for – us. Not that human beings are universally marvellous and lovely, of course, and not that we should judge by appearances… I'm going to stop talking now and do some breathing instead, if you don't mind.'

'Fine by me,' Emily whispered. Leaning

forwards on the console, she called out, 'We're scared, you know. Both of us are scared. We don't know where we are and we don't know what you want from us. Your standing out there isn't helping much! If we've disturbed you, we're sorry. We can't hurt you and don't want to hurt you.'

'*Hurt…*' said the voice.

'I hope it won't, you know, *fixate* on that,' Rory muttered.

'We don't want to be here,' Emily went on, 'and we'd rather leave you in peace.'

'*Peace…*'

There was a silence. The voice added nothing more, and its owner made no move.

'Sorry,' Emily said to Rory. 'Best I could do.'

He squeezed her hand. 'Brilliant job. The Doctor would be proud.'

'Who?'

'I've no idea. It just… came out.' But he didn't get a chance to chase that thought further. The owner of the voice entered the room.

He was a young man of about seventeen, with reddish hair, his cowlick slicked back inexpertly, and the merest makings of a moustache. He was in his shirt sleeves. He wore thick boots, and his trousers, held up by braces,

were patched and muddy. Seeing him, Emily
gave a loud, nervy laugh.

'Oh, Harry, you daft article, you've given us
ever such a fright! Why didn't you say hello?
Didn't you hear my voice? It's Emily! Emily
Bostock!'

The young man walked forwards until he
was standing at the top of the stairway leading
down to the console.

'My word,' Emily said, coming out from the
cover of the console. 'I should clout you!' She
turned to Rory, a smile upon her face. 'Don't
worry, Mr Williams, it's only Harry. Harry
Thompson. You remember? The one we saw in
the pictures.'

There was something not right here, Rory
thought, as Harry began to descend the steps.
Perhaps it was just the light, but the young
man's flesh had a yellowish tint, tinged with
green, and his eyes... His eyes were cold and
dark and lonely as a winter night.

'Emily,' Rory said quickly. 'Don't go any
closer.'

'Why ever not? I told you – this is Harry!
We've known each other all our lives. He
wouldn't hurt us!'

The young man was now at the bottom of the
steps. Emily reached out and took his hand. As

flesh met flesh, the lights all around began to flicker wildly. The throbbing sound, which had hitherto been no more than background noise, surged. The ship shuddered. Rory grabbed hold of the console with both hands.

'Emily! Get back!'

But Emily didn't seem in the least perturbed.

'Hush now,' she said, stroking the young man's hand. 'Everything's going to be all right. You don't have to be afraid. I won't tell on you, not for all the tea in China. I won't breathe a word. You're not going anywhere, Harry. You're not going anywhere you don't want to.'

But the lights were still flickering, Rory noticed, and the ship still shaking.

Jess finished her story, picked up her cup of tea, and looked over the rim of the mug across the table.

The two detectives stared back.

'I understand how it sounds,' Jess said patiently. 'But it's all true. Time pockets. Spatial ones too— Look, does either of you have a scarf?'

Neither of them responded. Jess sighed and drank some of the hot sweet tea. She was exhausted. Galloway had told her that only a few hours at the most had passed since she had parked her car on Long Lane and gone with Amy into the woods. By her own estimate, and even bearing in mind how time jumped around in Swallow Woods, Jess reckoned she and Vicky had taken the best part of two days to get from the clearing to the edge of the woods. For the last part of the journey, a storm had been chasing them, and it had been getting worse.

'It's all true,' she said, quietly but firmly. 'There's a clearing in the woods with paths running out from it. People get lost there, lost down pockets of time and space. It's been stable for a very long time, but now something's going wrong. I don't know what it is, but I do know that it's going to become critical tonight, and I do know that the town is at risk. What you have to do is let me talk to the Doctor.'

Galloway cleared his throat and leaned back in his chair. When he spoke, he used a very gentle tone that Jess, frankly, found pretty patronising.

'What I don't understand,' Galloway said, 'is that you must have met Laura Brown. She's a friend of your sister. You must want her to get home safe and sound—'

'Well of course I do! I want everyone in the town to be safe, and that's why you have to listen to me, Inspector! Listen to what I'm telling you!'

Galloway continued not to pay her any attention. 'I know that sometimes relationships between the press and the police can be tense, but you've always dealt fairly with me, and I feel as if I've always dealt fairly with you—'

'Yes, you've been marvellous! Wonderful! Brilliant! Now let me see the Doctor.'

'However,' Galloway went on, talking over her, 'even though you have clearly been through an unusual and probably distressing experience, you're running a risk of being charged with wasting police time.' He rubbed his temples. 'Did the red-haired girl put you up to this?'

'Amy? No! I told you – she's still in there! Look, if I could just speak to the Doctor—'

Galloway shook his head. 'Oh, no! Not a chance! He's obviously a very dangerous man, more dangerous than I thought already. I know the type – they have a twisted kind of charisma, they get other people to do their dirty work for them. Even sitting in the cells, he got the Pond girl to work on you. And now he seems to be controlling you in some way. For your own protection, Ms Ashcroft, you're not going anywhere near him!'

'For my own protection... Oh, for heaven's sake!' Jess gave up on Galloway and turned to the young female detective, who had been sitting silently throughout.

'It's Ruby Porter, isn't it?' Jess said. 'I knew your brother at school – James. He was great at cricket. Look, let's not waste any more time. We both know about the woods. We both know there's not a rational explanation for what happens – well, what we commonly understand as rational... Let's not complicate things right now. But you know, don't you, that there's something wrong with Swallow Woods. I can explain it, Ruby. Everything I'm saying is true!'

Porter looked away from her. She stared resolutely down at the floor. Jess now keenly understood the frustration that had made Amy tear at her hair.

'I know you've had a bad time,' Galloway said. 'It's unfortunate you can't bring yourself to be helpful right now, but at least you've confirmed my suspicion that whatever's going on here, the woods hold the key. At first light, I'm starting the search. It's not a big area. With police from three counties, local volunteers and the dog handlers, we'll soon find Ms Pond—'

'I wouldn't count on it!'

'—And we'll soon find out what's been going on in there.'

'Whatever's going on you're not equipped to deal with it! A search party? You think dogs can resolve this? This has been going on for centuries!' Jess stopped, backtracking slightly. 'Dogs... Like a hunt...' She addressed Galloway with new urgency. 'You know, I'm not sure taking dogs into Swallow Woods is a good idea—'

'I'm sure you don't,' said Galloway. He stood up to leave; Porter followed suit. 'Not right now. But you'll be glad in time.'

'No, really, don't do it!' Urgently, Jess turned to Porter. 'Listen to me! Please, you must understand! Something's going to happen tonight that could destroy the town. We don't know what it is yet, but I'm sure as I can be that dogs won't help. Hunted people fight back, they attack...! Please, if you won't let me talk to him, then you must! Talk to the Doctor!'

Galloway smiled benignly from the doorway. 'Drink up your tea, Ms Ashcroft. I'll get a car to take you home.'

Laura and the were-fox, who introduced himself as Reyn, led Amy inside to a big and comfortably appointed chamber. Long, high windows at the far end let sunlight stream in, and at the centre of the room was a large wooden table laid for supper. When she turned her head to look round, Amy thought she could see faint trails of golden shimmering light at the corner of her eye, like pollen drifting through the air.

'Come and eat,' said Laura, mistress of the house.

Amy went slowly towards the table, keeping a close watch on Reyn. He was walking lightly beside her, at her pace, and seemed prepared to let Laura do the talking. It was difficult to judge with a different species, but from the white hairs above each of his orange eyes, and his rather stately way of moving, Amy got the impression of an older man, even elderly. In fact, the pair of them – Laura and Reyn – struck Amy as being rather like an old couple who had been companions for a long time and were very comfortable with each other. Reyn went to the head of the table and waited politely for the two women to sit, one on either side of him.

'Were you lost for long?' Laura said.

'Not really,' Amy replied. 'A couple of hours, maybe?'

'Very quick! I must have wandered for at least two days.' Laura smiled as if the memory was somehow fond. 'Of course, it was all a very long time ago. It's almost as if it happened to somebody else.'

'About that,' said Amy. 'Weren't you…'

'Younger?'

'Yeah…' Amy fumbled around for a way to break the news.

'Don't torment yourself, Amy. I know that ten days have passed outside Swallow Woods since I walked under the trees. And, before you ask, sixty-one. Sixty-one years have passed here.'

That made her nearly eighty. 'Still,' Amy said feebly, 'you're looking good on it.'

'Thank you. Yes, I think I've weathered rather well.' Laura gestured around the table. 'Please, won't you eat?'

Reyn had not held back while they were talking. His plate was piled high with food and he was enjoying it. He tore into a chicken leg with great enthusiasm, stopping every couple of bites to dab a linen napkin against his mouth and wipe his fingers. It was an odd mixture of ferocity and fastidiousness. Laura gave him an indulgent smile.

Amy took a sample bite of bread and butter. The taste was odd, very bland at first, and then it was as if the flavour remembered to kick in, and her mouth was flooded with sensations of warm, nutty bread and creamy, salty butter.

'I have to say,' she said to Laura through a mouthful of cheese, 'You seem pretty laid back for someone who's been held captive for six decades.'

'Captive?' Laura gave a good-humoured snort, to which Reyn lent his odd rasping, coughing laugh. Laura reached out and took hold of his hand. 'Do you hear that? She thinks you're holding me captive!'

'You have to admit, lady, that you made the same mistake yourself, once upon a time.'

Laura gave him a fond smile.

Amy put down her fork. All this mutual admiration was starting to make her feel slightly nauseous. She sincerely hoped that she and Rory weren't like this. The thought of Rory made her anxious and perhaps even, though she didn't like to admit it, scared. Crossly, she said, 'OK, you two, tell me what's going on. Reyn's ship crashed here, didn't it? That's what's causing all the time pockets and disappearances. So how come it's not his fault?'

Laura and Reyn looked at her in surprise.

'Yes,' Reyn said. 'Yes, my ship crashed here. I've not had the resources or the right equipment to fix it. But rest assured, Amy, if I had my way

I would have left your planet centuries ago. I'm not a monster. I certainly wouldn't hold anyone against their will.'

'But all the missing people!' Amy said. 'Not just Laura – there've been hundreds!'

'Three hundred and nine, to be exact,' Reyn said. 'And not all of them have been as lucky as Laura.'

'*Lucky*? Oh yeah, she seems a real lottery winner to me!'

'Please, Amy,' Laura put in quietly. 'Let Reyn explain. 'When he does, you'll understand. There's no malice at work here. Just chance turnings on the road, and some bad luck – and,' she squeezed Reyn's hand, 'no small measure of happiness, in the end.'

'All right,' Amy said. 'I'm open to explanations. Just make them good.'

'I shall endeavour to do my best,' Reyn replied drily. Pouring out pale yellow wine for them all, he leaned back in his chair, goblet in hand, lord of the manor. 'I was an explorer, Amy. My ship could cross space as if it were no distance at all… Laura, my dear, do you have a skein of wool to hand so I might demonstrate?'

'Don't worry,' said Amy. She tapped her forehead. 'I've got the basics sorted.'

Reyn studied her thoughtfully. 'Laura, does

she strike you as remarkably at ease with the notion of space travel? And, indeed, at meeting a shape-shifting alien?'

'If something has happened in the outside world to make her like this,' Laura said, slowly coring an apple, 'it's happened in the last ten days.'

'Yeah, well, don't worry about me,' Amy said. 'I've been around a bit, that's all you need to know. Right now we're talking about where *you* came from. Your ships can travel through space. Yeah, great, I'm with you there. Spaceships – no problem. Massive fantasy castles and disappearing people – slightly more of a problem. So keep on with the explaining.'

Reyn bowed his head. 'As you command.'

'And you can drop the whole Camelot shtick too. Let's keep the talk straightforward, OK?'

Reyn's long ears twitched and flattened back slightly. 'Very well. Our exploration ships, Amy, were unusual in that they learned from their travels. In time they came to consciousness.'

'Yeah yeah, artificial intelligence, I'm fine with that too. Honestly, you're not likely to say something I haven't come across before in some shape or form. How has that ended up in mass kidnappings?'

'The process – we call it the Shift – is a

difficult transition, a vast and destabilising change. At home, we have teachers, scientists, all kinds of people to nurture them through the process. We can feed them information, show them experiences, give them all the knowledge we have accumulated. But my poor ship…' He sighed. 'When I crashed here in the woods, there were no people. I struggled to fix the ship with the resources I had. Before I could do that, the people came. It triggered the Shift.'

'How?' Amy said. 'How does that work?'

'During the Shift, the ship devours information. When the people came through the woods, it took them. You have to understand, Amy, it was acting on instinct. It was trying to learn. Every fifty years or so, the ship needs more. Every fifty years or so, it would pull people to it. It wants memories, experiences, life stories.' He looked away. 'It's not painful, Amy, but it's hardly desirable. Whenever the ship has pulled people into the wood, I've tried to bring them here instead. I've not always been successful.'

Jess and Vicky, Amy thought. *Rory…* She pushed her plate aside and put her head in her hands.

'Laura I was able to save,' Reyn said. 'And you, now. Your two companions…' He shook his head. 'I wish you'd been able to bring yourself to trust me. But there it is. My appearance, I have gathered over the years, does not always encourage that. I've tried to make this place beautiful and comfortable for all my guests, as welcoming as possible – but your species can be so suspicious! It's not our way. We're curious, like you, but not so mistrustful. Perhaps that's a failing.'

'You said that you've brought many people here over the years,' Amy said thickly. 'There was a young man came this way, about a century ago in Laura's time. He would have complained a lot—'

'He didn't come this way, I'm afraid. If he passed in summer through the glade in the wood with the pool, he most likely found himself on board the ship.' He studied her with his orange eyes, seeming to understand that this was someone important. 'I'm sorry, Amy.'

Amy shoved her chair back and stood up. She started pacing around the room, coming to a halt near the long windows. Rain was pattering against the panes. She swung back round to face Reyn and Laura. They were sitting watching her, obviously concerned.

'You say you don't have the equipment to fix your ship,' Amy said. 'So why not just let this

Shift or whatever it is finish, and then get out of here! Leave the town and the people in peace!'

'It's not that simple—'

'Oh,' Amy muttered through her teeth, 'I just *knew* you were going to say that…'

'At home, as I said, we have all kinds of experts to hand. Here, there's only me. And there's more. As the years have passed, the ship has become more bound to the world around it, more entangled with it. All the warps and pockets have become so complex that if I tried now to make the ship shift completely, if I tried to force it through – I don't know what damage that would do.'

Amy turned back to the window. The rain was falling steadily now, and some of the water was leaking through and gathering in a small pool at the base of the window. Why would you make it rain, she wondered, in a fantasy world? Perhaps sunshine became boring after a while. Perhaps you started to crave some darkness, some semblance of risk.

'Something's going to happen soon,' she said. 'I don't know what, but this time next week, there'll be a lake covering Swallow Woods, and nothing where the town once stood. Is that what could happen if the Shift was forced?'

'Yes,' said Reyn, speaking slowly. 'How

161

do you know that, Amy? What makes you so sure?'

'Don't bother about that. Just give me answers. What could make that happen?'

Reyn didn't reply at once. When Amy turned around, she saw Laura leaning across, holding the alien's hand, her eyes pleading with him to speak.

'Tell me,' Amy said. 'I'm not afraid of the truth. What might cause the ship to shift?'

'I've maintained the balance for centuries now, Amy,' Reyn said, 'but it's very delicate. The ship might come to a crisis if there were too many people trying to get in at once. But the real risk comes from people trying to get out. Trying to leave through the portal place.'

'The portal place?'

'The clearing in the wood with the pool. Where we met. That's where your world ends and mine begins.'

'And coming through there,' Amy said, 'brings you either here or to the ship.'

'That's right.'

'And going back out again—'

'Could destabilise the environment I've set up here, and bring on exactly the kind of crisis I've been trying to stop. That's why I've never left your world. That's why nobody leaves.'

'I told you I wasn't a captive,' Laura Brown said softly, 'but I can't go back from here. This is where all our journeys end, Amy. There's no way back through Swallow Woods. Not if we are all to survive.'

Porter saw Galloway safely out of the station on his way back to Swallow Woods, and then quietly, and unnoticed, she slipped down to the cells.

The station was almost deserted; everyone was home or else down at the search. The sergeant led her down the bare bright corridor to the cell, and Porter waited patiently while he unlocked it. The strip light above them fizzled.

'Been like that all night,' the sergeant complained. 'Can't stand fluorescents. Susceptible to bad weather.'

Porter made vague noises of agreement as he opened the cell door. 'Very quiet, this one,' he said. 'Almost too quiet. You'd think he'd ask for a cup of tea at some point, but, no, all he wanted was the spoon.'

The door swung opened. Porter looked past the sergeant into the cell.

The Doctor was standing on the bed with one hand aloft. In that hand, he was holding up the spoon so that it touched the ceiling. The other hand was covering his left ear. Seeing the pair at the door, his expression turned from intense concentration to faint embarrassment. He brought down his arm and jumped from the bed.

'Sorry. Had to do some… important… spoon work.' Carefully, he handed the piece of cutlery over to the sergeant. 'Thanks for that. Good spoon. One of the best.'

The sergeant gave Porter a 'he's all yours' look, and left them alone.

Porter leaned in the doorway, arms folded, blocking the exit. 'All right,' she said. 'What's going on?'

'You already know what's going on. Aliens. Starships. Space bending back round on itself. Time, too. But you're in luck. Help is here.' He gave a bright smile; did jazz hands. 'Where's your friend?'

'He's off to search the woods. With dogs.'

'Ooh, no, terrible idea! Who knows what that will do? Some people can get very testy, particularly when they've been on their own for a long time. Dogs send the wrong message, don't they?'

'That's why I'm here,' Porter said. 'Jess said—'

'Oh, Jess made it! Excellent! What about

Pond, was she with her?'

'No sign of her, not yet.'

The Doctor's face fell. 'Ah. Well. At least Jess is a start. But there's still Amy, and Rory, and Emily, and of course the small matter of whatever minor apocalypse is about to hit Foxton; just because it's only going to affect one small town and an equally small woodland area doesn't make it less of an apocalypse for the people concerned – not to mention that if the motorway gets flooded the traffic is going to be appalling throughout the rest of the county for who knows how long— Sorry. Talk too much. Always did. You were saying?'

'Jess said that you knew about...' Porter stopped, as if having difficulty saying the words.

'Say it,' suggested the Doctor. 'You'll feel so much better when you do.'

'About the woods,' Porter said, in a rush. 'You know what happens when people disappear in Swallow Woods.'

The Doctor smiled at her, gently, kindly. 'Yes, you knew, didn't you? Detective Constable Porter, who has lived in this town all her life, and can hear the same noise that I can hear, and who knows that there's something not right about the woods. Something that can't be solved by ordinary methods – not even by a hard-working, fair-minded, and meticulous policeman. And particularly not by his dogs. Who went missing? Somebody close to you?'

Porter looked past him, over at the wall. 'My mother's older brother. My uncle, of course – although that's not how you think of a 15-year-old boy.'

'When did it happen?'

'About… 1960? No, 1959. That fits with the dates, doesn't it? Every fifty years, give or take a few years. At least, I think that's right – people round here don't exactly talk openly about all this. He was the only one that time. Gran never got over it. Sometimes she would be so sad. Right to the end of her life…' Porter stared up at the little window on the far wall, dark and wet with rain. 'Sadness like that, it gets handed down, doesn't it? Even though I never knew him – my mother hardly remembers him – you still get touched by the sadness. He's why I joined the police. Always wanting to find lost things, always wanting to put things right…' She shook her head. 'It's not just me. The whole town is like that! There's a strange sense of loss that comes from living here in Foxton. It's like something has always been missing, but you don't dare to remember what it was.

You're always thinking about it, but you know you wouldn't go looking, because in your heart you know that the answers can only be found in Swallow Woods. And who goes near Swallow Woods? If you go there, you might not find your way out again. You'd be lost too, and perhaps people wouldn't quite remember you either. Poor Gordon Galloway. I bet he's sorry he ever moved down here.'

The Doctor, she realised, was standing very close to her.

'I can end this,' he told her softly. 'Whatever has been happening here for such a long time, I can end it. No more disappearances, no more secrets and fears and half-truths and confusion. I can end it all tonight. But I can't end it from here.'

Porter looked anxiously over her shoulder.

'It's coming to an end anyway,' the Doctor said. 'The choice now is between the happy ending or the tragedy. But this is when you make a decision, Detective. You can play by the rules, the old rules, the ones that have kept this town terrified for so long, nobody talking about what happens – or you can take a risk. Admit that what's been going on all these years is real. Bewildering, inexplicable – but *real*.'

Porter was listening to him as if mesmerised.

'I've been watching you a lot the last day or so,' she said, slowly.

'You should see me in a fez. Looks *good*...'

'I couldn't make sense of your eyes. You don't look old. Except for your eyes. What do they see, Doctor?'

'Bad things, cruel things. Terrible things made all the worse by how beautiful they are. And sometimes – yes, often, because the universe is full of wonders as well as terrors – the most marvellous thing that it's possible to see. Someone opening her mind.'

'All right,' said Porter. 'I know you're just reeling me in, but whatever you're doing, it works. I'll get you out of the station, and then you're on your own.' She put her hands to her head and sighed. 'What am I doing? I *like* my job!'

'There's one more thing I need,' said the Doctor.

'What more do you want?'

'There's a widget. A gadget. A *thing*. About so long.' He pulled his hands apart about eight inches. 'Green light at the end. Makes a funny noise... You know, I'm fairly certain that you'll recognise it when you see it.'

The strip light in the corridor wavered perilously. Outside, the wind was howling.

'Thirdly,' said the Doctor, 'and, I promise that this is finally – might I also ask for some *haste*?'

Chapter
11

When the meal was finished, Reyn lifted his hand and, with one wave, the room around them disappeared, leaving only faint golden trails behind it. A new room formed around them; a pleasant chamber with a fire crackling at one end, and two chairs by the hearth. Laura sat down in one of these, and took out a rich piece of embroidery from a workbox at her feet. Reyn bowed to Amy, and left.

Amy stalked restlessly around the room like a wild animal trapped in a cage. The air had an odd flavour – stale, metallic – and she could not shake the feeling of being enclosed in a small space. When she ran her finger against surfaces – the tapestries, the thick stone walls of the castle – flecks of light gathered and followed her fingertip wherever she traced with it. Whatever tricks Reyn pulled to give the illusion of space, there were clearly limits to his abilities.

Reaching the window, Amy tugged at the curtains. Night had fallen and it was pitch black outside. That only added to her sense of claustrophobia. She abandoned her progress round the room and slumped into the chair opposite Laura. She nodded down at her needlework.

'So is that how you've filled the time?'

'Hardly!'

'So what have you been doing with yourself for the past, ooh, six decades?'

Laura calmly completed a few more stitches before answering. 'At first, I tried to get away. You wouldn't believe how many times I tried to get away! How many different routes I tried! Of course, I always ended up back in the glade. That's where all the paths lead – the great green cathedral of trees. And Reyn was always there, to bring me home.'

'I bet he was,' Amy muttered.

'After a while it seemed stupid to waste so much energy and emotion on a pointless activity. Particularly when there were so many marvels here to see. Thread this needle for me, will you, Amy? My eyes aren't what they were.'

Amy squinted, and poked the loose end through the eye of the needle with one quick stab. As she bit off the thread, she said, 'What marvels are you talking about? What is there to see here? You're stuck in the middle of a wood!'

'You saw the valley!' Laura said. 'You saw how beautiful it is here! And this is only the most recent of the worlds we've lived in. Reyn can create whatever I want, whatever I imagine! Space stations, intergalactic empires, a gothic mansion filled with spooks and ghouls, our own world at any time in its history!'

'Yes, but it's all fake, isn't it?' Amy waved her hand quickly to and fro, and a trail of golden light followed the movement. 'I don't know how he does it – virtual reality, maybe, or a simulation, or something to do with him being a shape-shifter… Oh, I don't know! I *do* know that none of it is real! It's horrible! It's like you've been stuck in a role-playing game your whole life!' She leaned forwards in her chair. 'Laura, I've seen marvels – *real* marvels – things I can touch and smell and taste, and I haven't had to be stuck in the same place in order to see them! My friend – the Doctor – he's taken me to places you wouldn't believe!'

'Then you of all people should understand, Amy. Of anyone that's ever come this way – you should understand! That's exactly what Reyn has done for me! Perhaps aliens and starships and walking through a door out onto a different world isn't anything particularly wonderful for you, but it was for me! To think that I once thought I might make it as far as Africa!'

'You're not even five miles from home! You're trapped!'

'Trapped is a state of mind. If we thought that way, we wouldn't be able to bear it—'

'Er, excuse me – there's no "we" about this! I'm not staying here a moment longer than I can help. First light – I'm out of here!'

Laura gave the kind of smile that can only infuriate. 'We'll see. We'll see.'

At this point, Reyn came back into the room. He crossed over to the fire, carrying a third chair with him, and sat warming his hands. In the candlelight, there was a real beauty to him – the thick, well-kept reddish hair; the sad, clever, orange eyes; the melancholy that seemed to gather around him like the light that followed Amy's finger... Amy shook herself. No, she wasn't going to be charmed by this creature, however beautiful and lonely and persuasive he might be.

Reyn had become aware that she was watching him. His ears twitched back. 'I do understand your frustration, Amy,' he said, 'but I cannot risk lowering the barriers around the portal place. It's too dangerous.'

Amy nodded towards the door. 'Were you standing out there listening for long?'

'I think you already know that this place is not as large as the impression might give. I could hear your voice quite clearly in the next tower.'

Amy blushed with embarrassment. 'Sorry,' she said. 'Didn't mean to shout. Still, why can't I try? Isn't it always worth trying?'

'I lost count of the number of times I tried, Amy,' Laura said. 'We're only trying to save you a great deal of heartbreak.'

'It's true,' Reyn said, 'that I cannot be entirely sure what would happen if I let you through, Amy. It may make no difference at all. But my best guess – and it's an educated guess – is that it would bring on the Shift. That puts the town at risk. I am the one responsible here, and I don't think that's a risk worth taking.'

'Is this place really so terrible, Amy?' Laura said. 'Could you not at least wait for a while and see? It might be more bearable than you're imagining.'

And, for a moment, sitting in that comfortable chair by that warm and lovely fire, Amy was tempted. Would it be so bad, after all, to stay here, in this calm, beautiful place, in this gentle kindly company; to leave whatever disaster was unfolding to somebody else to deal with? This place was enclosed, secluded – perhaps even if Swallow Woods did flood and become covered in water, this place would remain intact, sealed away. She might be safe here.

But she wouldn't be with Rory, and she wouldn't be Amy Pond.

'It's no use,' Amy said. 'I have to take the risk. I know something's going to happen soon that will destroy the town and flood the valley. But I don't really know what causes it. What if it's because I *don't* try to get out? I don't know whether the Doctor is free or not, I don't know whether Jess and Vicky made it, and I don't know what Rory is doing right now, whenever he is. I do know that I can't sit around waiting for events to catch up with me. I have to do *something*,' she said, 'and then take the consequences. I'll wait till first light, and then I'll go.'

'But you won't get through,' Reyn said. 'I can't let you get through.'

'And I can't *not* try! First light, I'm off.'

Reyn sighed. 'Here, of course, we don't have to wait for dawn to arrive. We can bring it to us.'

He waved his hand. Amy got up, crossed to the window, and pulled the curtains back. Already the sky was pale and, quickly, it was suffused with a golden haze. Then the yellow sun emerged. This all took the matter of a moment.

'Whatever it is you're doing here,' Amy told Reyn, 'it's pretty impressive.'

'Thank you,' Reyn replied. 'I've had a long time to perfect it. Shall we go?'

In the courtyard, the sun was already high overhead. Laura laid her hand, parchment thin with age, upon Amy's cheek. 'Don't be too heartbroken if you find yourself back here with us,' she said. 'I've had a good life, and a happy one.'

'I won't be back,' Amy said. 'But I'll tell your parents you said that, if you like.'

Laura's face crinkled up with an old but unforgotten pain. 'Don't,' she said. 'I know you mean well, but don't hold out hopes like that.'

Reyn bent to kiss his lady's hand and then, in the blink of an eye, he and Amy were standing once again on the edge of the wood. Looking back down into the valley, Amy saw Laura's castle. A soft spring rain was falling, and a double rainbow had formed across the bowl of the valley, brightly coloured and essentially ephemeral.

'Good luck,' Reyn said. 'Although I think it won't be long before you're back with us again.'

'Nothing ventured,' Amy said, and plunged back underneath the dark cover of the trees.

As Emily kept speaking, her words seemed to have a soothing effect not just on Harry, but even on the ship. The lights settled down and the noise fell back to its gentlest hum. Best of all, from Rory's perspective, the walls stopped shaking.

'There,' Emily said. 'No need for us all to get so worked up. I told you, it's only Harry. Oh, but Harry, have you been here by yourself all this time? Did you get lost?'

'*Lost*…' whispered the young man. '*Lost*…'

'Eh, now, come on, Harry, I know you must have been scared – heaven knows me and Mr Williams have been – but can't you even manage a hello? We're old friends, aren't we?'

'Emily,' said Rory. 'I'm not sure that's Harry.'

'What? Don't be daft – look at him! You saw

his picture over there! Besides, I've known Harry Thompson since he was toddling round our yard. I'd recognise him anywhere!'

'What I mean is, it might *look* like Harry, and it might even be his body, but...' Rory struggled to explain. 'It's not him inside.'

'Well, that's just a load of old nonsense.' Emily stared into her friend's eyes and squeezed his hand again. 'You're there, Harry, aren't you? You've just had a shock.' To Rory, she said, 'Given you don't know what a white feather is, or a conchie, do you think it's possible you might not recognise shellshock when you see it? Well, I can, and that's what it looks like to me. Harry's here, aren't you, love? We've just got to find a way to make you feel safe again.'

'*Safe... Safe...*'

Emily made Harry sit down on the steps. She knelt down in front of him, putting his hands within hers. 'Can you tell us what happened, love? Can you remember?'

'*Remember...*' The young man's eyes came sharply into focus. He stared so hard at Emily that Rory was suddenly afraid for her. He reached forwards to try to disentangle their hands, but Emily shook him off.

'We're getting there,' she said. 'He'll be talking soon. Isn't that better than running around getting nowhere?'

'Remember…' Harry's voice was getting steadily stronger. 'The long journey… The dark, the cold… Saw light! Felt something… something new… Pain…'

'I know, love,' Emily said consolingly. 'Go on, now, you'll feel better once you've let it all out.'

'Needed rest. Needed time… to *think*!' The young man's voice became suddenly excited. 'To know! To grow! To become… to become *different*…'

'Eh, now, love, you're not making much sense.'

'Emily,' Rory said quickly. 'Wait a minute. Look – I think I might know what's happening here. A dark journey? That's not how it was for us, is it? We came through bright sunshine, remember?'

'Yes, but you said the place could change—'

'Can I have a go? Can I talk to him? I promise I won't say anything to upset him.'

Emily looked at him doubtfully. 'Well, all right then, but be kind.'

Rory knelt down in front of the young man. 'Your long cold journey,' he said, 'were there stars?'

'Stars… suns… worlds… Then the pain. Then

this world. Fell here. The pain too much… Still wanting to know, to see, to learn… So much here to know, to learn… So much… Soon be ready… Soon be… Soon be me!'

'Mr Williams, I'm not sure it helps sending him off on flights of fancy like this—'

'One more question, Emily, I promise.' Again Rory addressed the young man. 'What have you learned? Who did you learn it from?'

Emily frowned at him. 'Eh?'

'Just let him answer, Emily. Then I'll know for sure.'

The young man looked at Rory. His eyes were vacant and unfocused.

'What did you learn?' Rory said again. 'Who taught you?'

'They came here. There were none before. Then they came. They love and live and quarrel and die in less time than it takes for a tree to grow. They are like the leaves. They are cruel and kind and brave and afraid. Sometimes they know no better. Sometimes they are at fault. Sometimes they doubt. Sometimes they believe. And always they want to know…'

'Mr Williams, I don't understand all this—'

'Doesn't sound much like Harry Thompson any more, does it?' Turning back to Harry once again, Rory said, 'How many? How many have come here?'

'One hundred and seventy-three,' the young man rattled off promptly, like a machine reading out data.

Rory recoiled. There was a sick taste in his mouth. 'A hundred and seventy-three!'

Emily pulled at his arm. 'You'd better start explaining things, mister, or else I'm going to start getting right ticked off with you.'

'How many pictures did we count, Emily?'

'What?'

'On the screen over there. How many different people?'

'More than a hundred, I reckon. We never got to the end, did we? What are you saying, Mr Williams?'

'This isn't Harry,' Rory said. He stood up, and turned away, repulsed. He ran down to the console, waving it back to life, and he started hunting, certain now that he would eventually find what he was looking for.

'All these *people*!' he said, as the images rushed past. 'They came this way, and it took their memories! Emily, that might be Harry's body, but it's certainly not Harry that's talking to us. It's the ship!'

Rory looked down at the console. He waved his hand and stopped the flow of pictures. The blow on the head hadn't taken his memories away. There he was, on the screen, surrounded by impenetrable text. 'It takes memories! The ship steals memories! My memories!'

In the foyer of the police station, Jess watched the storm and waited for the car to arrive to take her home. As the wind hammered at the roof, Galloway came through the double doors that led back into the main part of the building. He stood for a moment peering unhappily out at the rain running in rivulets down the window. Then he pulled out a newspaper and shook it out to use as an umbrella.

It was worth one last try. 'Please,' Jess said. 'Don't search the woods. Talk to the Doctor first—'

'I have talked to him. All I want to know is where he's keeping Laura Brown. Unfortunately, he had nothing useful to say.' Galloway pushed open the entrance doors. 'Go home, Ms Ashcroft. Get a good night's sleep. Call me tomorrow once you've had a chance to think – and if you've anything sensible to say.'

He ducked out into the rain. It was lashing down now, a real storm. Jess watched the inspector sprint across to his car, holding his copy of *The Herald* over his head. There was a flash of lightning followed by a long roll of thunder so loud it almost seemed to make the ground shudder. This, Jess thought, desperately, was how it would feel at the end of the world. Soon the dogs would be going into the woods, yelling, barking, on the hunt for the strange fox creature that she had surely seen…

Behind her, the officer at the desk, in a doubtful voice, said, 'Inspector Galloway didn't mention anything about it…'

'No?' A young female voice. 'Well, he was quite clear in his instructions to me.'

Jess looked round. There was Ruby Porter, a study in nonchalance. Standing behind her…

The   Doctor,   handcuffed,   and uncharacteristically meek.

'He's wanted down at the search,' Porter went on. 'If we really *are* going to search the woods,' she and the officer shook their heads at outsiders who insisted on blundering about near Swallow Woods, 'then I suppose we'd better do it properly.' At this point, Porter noticed Jess. 'How about I give Ms Ashcroft that lift home at the same time? Save you the bother of rustling up a car.'

Now that Porter had given him a solution to his small but immediately pressing problem, the officer was much more willing to let the pair past. Pushing the Doctor ahead of her, Porter walked over to the doors.

'Follow me,' she muttered to Jess on her way past. Jess dutifully obeyed. Porter led them through the rain towards a little dark blue car. 'In the back, both of you,' she hissed.

Jess opened the back door and shoved the Doctor in, hurrying after him and shaking the water from her hair as soon as she was inside. Porter, getting into the driver's seat, said, 'I suppose I'm going to get disciplined for this. At the very least. Probably fired.'

'Cheer up!' the Doctor said. 'Might never happen! Might not get the chance. After all, it's entirely possible that this time next week the town won't be here any longer. Under those circumstances, I seriously doubt anyone would have disciplinary procedures on their mind—'

Porter, furiously, started the car.

'Doctor—' Jess said, urgently.

He raised his cuffed hands to stop her. 'The word you are looking for,' he said, 'is were-fox.' He leaned forwards to address Porter. 'Constable,' he said, 'the gadget with the green light. Did you have any success in… umgph!'

The end of his sentence was lost. Porter had shoved the sonic screwdriver between his teeth, without taking her eyes off the road. The Doctor turned and dropped the device into Jess's lap.

'Ms Ashcroft,' he said politely, holding up his cuffed hands and nodding down at the sonic. 'That button, there— No, *there*. Yes! That's the one!'

'It's not Harry talking to us,' Rory said. 'It's the ship! It takes memories! The ship steals memories. My memories!'

It was as if the ship heard him speak. Once again, the walls shuddered, with even more force, and the body-that-was-once-Harry convulsed. Emily put her arm around the boy's shoulder.

'Stolen your memories?' she snapped. 'Nonsense! You got a tap on the head, that's all! Not stolen any of mine, has it?'

'Perhaps it can only cope with one person at a time. Perhaps you're next! Oh, I don't know, Emily, I'm not the memory-stealing spaceship!'

'Anyway, how can a man be a ship? That's like saying he's a motor car or a train!'

'It's using his body as a kind of transmitter…' Rory cast around for an example she might understand. 'Like he's a walking telegram! He's carrying messages from the ship to us. He's the means by which the ship is able to talk to us.'

'Well, if he's passing on messages, that's good, isn't it? We'll be able to talk to the ship, maybe ask it to let us go home?'

'You don't understand – the ship isn't *asking* him to pass on messages. It's *making* him do it.'

'Eeuw!' said Emily. 'That's horrible!' Her hold on Harry's hand got tighter. 'But is Harry still in there? Are you there, love? Can you hear me?'

'I don't think he can be there. I think the ship has taken his memories, like it's taken some of mine—'

'Poor thing!' said Emily, and from the way she was stroking Harry's hand, Rory got the distinct impression she wasn't talking about him.

'Er, excuse me? My memories too? Pinched? Stolen? Not here?'

'Oh, yes, but look – you're still intact, aren't you? Still standing, still talking. Whereas Harry can't remember a thing, and as for the ship... Well, you heard it! All that talk of learning, and growing – it sounds like a child to me.'

'Pinched!' Rory tapped the side of his head. 'Stolen! No longer there! Honestly, what does somebody have to do to get some sympathy around here?'

'I'm not saying it's not horrible for you, just

that I don't think it knew any better.'

'That's all very well for you to say, Emily, but it's not your memories that have been stolen! And it's not you that could have been turned into a walkie-talkie!'

'A whichety-what?' Emily shook her head. 'You do talk some nonsense! And look! You're upsetting him!' She put her arm around Harry, who was shaking violently. 'Hush, love, it's all right!'

'Me? Upsetting *him*? Anyway, him – it's not a him, it's an it! And what about all the people it's taken? Too right it should be upset! It should be very upset! Not to mention ashamed!'

Harry – or the ship – began to moan, a low drone pitched at the same level as the engine's throb, like the wind howling round a wasteland.

'Oh, do stop! Look what you're doing to him!' Emily patted the young man's hand. 'Shush now! Don't you worry! It's not your fault.'

'Er, well, actually, it *is* its fault. One hundred and seventy-three times over. All those people! It doesn't bear thinking about... What did it *do* with them? Did they spend their days like Harry here, stolen from their friends and their family, walking around this tiny ship like... like *zombies*! It's awful, Emily! And it could have happened to us! It could have taken us! It's already taken some of my memories! Did I mention that? My memories? Taken?'

'*Taken…*' whispered the ship, in Harry's voice. '*Stolen… Lost…*' Slowly, tears began to roll down the young man's cheeks. Once again, the walls around them shook hard, as if a deep and guilty wave of sorrow was passing through them.

'Don't, Mr Williams! Please! Can't you see you're distressing it? It's like bullying a child!' To the young man, the young ship, Emily said, 'Don't listen to him, love! Here, what should I call you? If you're not really Harry? Do you have a name? Can you tell me? No? Ship sounds so funny, but I suppose it'll have to do. Don't upset yourself, Ship. You didn't know what you were doing. Now you know, you can stop, can't you?'

'Maybe it can stop, but it can't take back what it's done,' Rory pointed out. And with another deep sigh of shuddering grief, Ship said:

'Sorry… Sorry to be… Sorry to be born…'

It shook again. The lights on the walls dimmed and flickered. This time some patches stayed dark, and others turned an alarming red. The hum rose in pitch and volume, the unmistakable sound of an alarm, like a wind howling through the trees.

'Can't you see what you're doing?' Emily said to Rory. 'You're hurting it! For all we know you could be killing it! What happens to us then, Mr Williams? What happens to us all then?'

A great gale tore through Swallow Woods. The trees shook and threw whatever they could into the path of Amy Pond. She ducked to avoid a branch that flung itself at her, and ran on. There was a grey patch of light ahead. Amy chased it—

And came out into the glade, the portal place, the ancient green chapel where all paths led. She could distinguish no season here now. The rain lashed down, the trees rocked to and fro as if in pain, and, in the centre of the clearing, the water in the pool was rising. In the distance, faintly, Amy heard the barking of dogs.

'Got to go,' Amy told herself. 'Got to get out!'

She ran beneath one of the great silent arches, the storm battering her. A few minutes later – breathless, exhausted, soaked to the skin – she saw another grey slab of light…

And came back into the clearing, where the trees were writhing and the water still rising. Again, she tried – ran through beating rain with the yell of hounds ringing in her ears – and again she got no further than the glade. The pool was swollen, overflowing, the water lapping almost at her ankles now. This, surely, was the start of whatever disaster was going to befall Swallow Woods and the people of Foxton. Amy had tried her best, but either it had not been enough, or else it had been the last straw.

Teeth chattering, bitterly cold, Amy sank to the ground. The rain lashed against her face. She scrubbed at the water, and then saw, standing on the other side of the glade, framed by a swaying arch of old trees, Reyn.

'I truly am sorry,' he said, 'but I did not lie to you. You cannot leave Swallow Woods.'

'I must!' Amy yelled. 'I have to! There's nobody else!'

'But look around you, Amy! Look at what's happening!'

Thunder rolled and there was a flash of light. Torches? Searchlights? Lightning? Amy could not tell. She put her arms across her knees and dropped her head wearily down against them. 'There has to be a way. There *must* be!'

'I'm sorry, Amy,' Reyn said. 'There's no way through the woods.'

'Of course there's a way,' another voice said, a familiar voice that made Amy's heart somersault in her chest. 'There's always a way.'

It felt to Amy as if she had been locked in a deep dark dungeon, and somebody had thrown open the door, let in fresh air and bright sunlight, and then showed her that the key had been in her pocket all along. She leapt to her feet, and cried out in joy.

'Doctor!'

Chapter
12

There he was, the Doctor, leaning against a tree, chucking the sonic screwdriver up into the air and catching it, and looking very pleased with himself.

Amy ran over – and belted him on the arm. 'You took your time!'

'Ow! Don't be *too* excited about seeing me, will you?'

'I've been running around here like a hamster on a wheel, getting *soaked*... What have you been *doing*?'

'Breaking out of jail. I'm an outlaw now, Pond, a vagabond. A man on the run. I live on the edge, with only my wits and my trusty sonic screwdriver to keep me one step ahead of the law.'

'So they let you out?'

'It was in fact a touch more clandestine than that. There was actual stealth involved at one point – but, yes, broadly speaking, they let me out.'

'And Jess? What about Jess and Vicky? Did they get through?'

'They got through, just about…' The Doctor switched on the sonic, and waved it around vigorously and possibly even to some specific end. 'Ooh, I see! All got very complicated here, hasn't it? All these fixes and patches. And then three people come along at once! Ship and pilot were so busy with you, Amy, that Vicky and Jess were able to get past both of them… Look at these readings! Someone's not in as much control round here as he'd like to think. Speaking of whom…' he swung round and pointed the sonic at Reyn, 'are you going to introduce us, Amy?'

He was staring at the were-fox with the kind of look that he generally reserved for his more intractable foes.

'This is Reyn,' Amy said. 'Now don't go Time Lord on him. He didn't mean any harm…'

'They usually don't.'

'He's been stuck here too! He couldn't fix the ship and get away—'

'Fatalism. Dreadful habit. Leads to all kinds of vices, like trapping passing strangers in your timeless fantasy playground or not bothering to brush your teeth.'

'I think he's done his best with limited resources,' Amy said. 'No bad breath, at any rate.' She wiped her face. It was still raining heavily and from beyond the trees came a faint but persistent barking. 'Doctor, are you going to stand around being all Dark Knight about this for much longer? Or can we skip to the bit where we find out what's happening and then stop it?'

The Doctor popped his sonic screwdriver back into his pocket. 'I'm prepared to put things behind me. Let's see whether he is.' He walked across the clearing and gave Reyn an elaborate formal greeting which the were-fox, startled, reciprocated with great elegance.

'I know your species,' the Doctor said. 'I know your myths, your legends, your history. I know all about the Long War and what happened—' He stopped himself. 'Anyway, enough of my chit and chat – why don't you tell me what really brought your ship down here?'

Amy, confused, said, 'I thought he crashed?'

'Which I think is probably partly true,' said

the Doctor, 'but not entirely true. Am I right?'

Reyn, who had been watching the Doctor warily, nodded slowly. 'I was being chased by enemy gunships. I was attacked and my ship was damaged. That part was completely true. I intended to hide here until my ship was healed. Then the people came and the Shift got under way.'

'And that's when all this malarkey with the time pockets and the portal-building and the disappearances started, yes?'

'Doctor,' Amy said, 'hang on a minute…'

'Make up your mind, Pond! A moment ago you were telling me to hurry up!'

'Shut up.' She raised a warning finger. 'And fill me in on this Long War business, OK?'

'The worlds inhabited by Reyn's people, Amy, had – at one point in their history – the misfortune to find themselves living right next door to quite a substantial interplanetary empire. Empires are in general greedy beasts, and this one was no exception. You've seen the kinds of technology that Reyn has at his disposal, not to mention the shape-shifting. There was a war—'

'I'm guessing that it was a long war,' Amy said.

'It has been a very long war,' said Reyn.

'Several generations now.'

'And you've presumably worked out that they're rather a long-lived species,' said the Doctor. 'So you brought the ship down, Reyn, the Shift began but, given the damage done and your lack of support infrastructure, you've not been able either to fix the ship and leave, or else to shut it down entirely and stop people being taken. You've only been able to hold back the whole process. Yes, a very difficult situation…'

'I told you he'd been trying his best,' Amy said. Turning to Reyn, she asked, 'Why didn't you tell me all that earlier? About the war?'

Quietly, from behind her shoulder, the Doctor said, 'I suspect Reyn's enemies weren't only trying to find out how the ship worked, Amy. I rather imagine they wanted to study the shape-shifting too. I'd hide under those circumstances. I might not reveal too much about myself either.'

'And we're supposed to be the suspicious ones,' Amy said.

'I've learned the hard way,' Reyn replied. He sighed, deeply. 'I want to leave this world,' he said. 'More than anything! I want to get home, return to the struggle. I've been away far too long. But I'm stuck here. I have no way out. Either I maintain the environment I've created, or the ship shifts and the town and its people are lost. I brought us here! It's my responsibility. What choice do I have?'

He looked pathetic, the rain running down his red pelt, his ears flat and dejected. Amy put her hand upon his arm.

'So what you need,' the Doctor said thoughtfully, 'is help with the ship. If we can guide the ship successfully through its Shift, you and it would be free to leave—'

'Yes, but, as I've said – I can't maintain the integrity of this environment and handle the Shift! Not all at once! Something will give!'

'Yes, yes, that's what I'll help with! Hello! This is the help you've been waiting for all these years! Here I am! The help!' He gave a friendly little wave. 'I'll go to the ship. Children *love* me!'

'Doctor,' Amy hissed. 'What about Rory?'

'Ah, yes! The elusive Mr Pond. I wonder what he's been up to? Certainly not triangulating. Perhaps we should find out exactly what he's been doing for the past century with that delightful young woman. I imagine Reyn can help with that, guide me through to the ship at the right time. Rory and Emily can help me with the Shift, Reyn can maintain the environment, and when we're done, you can both set sail again and leave this poor old wood in peace to get on with making acorns and feeding squirrels and being a nice place to go for a picnic. Ha! How does that sound as a deal, Reyn? You get to leave, Swallow Woods gets picnickers, and we get Rory. Actually,' he looked excited, 'we might just have a picnic afterwards, too. So. What do you think?'

Reyn did not answer. Close by, dogs were barking.

'Listen,' said the Doctor. 'They're coming. The humans, their dogs. I've met the man in charge. He's a decent sort, but he's very cross right now. Things haven't been going his way recently. He's not in the mood for holding back. So whatever you decide, you'd better decide it soon. Those dogs are scary, and your ship might not wait for them to board it. Besides, I think the Shift is going to happen whether you like it or not. Look around. Look at what's happening.'

Amy saw that the trees were in chaos: all the seasons were jumbled up. Here, one tree was full of blossom and heavy with thick green leaves; there, another tree was bright with autumn colours. It seemed that the portal place was breaking down.

'Trust me,' said the Doctor. 'After all, I'll be trusting you with Amy.' He leaned sideways.

'You're all right with that, aren't you, Pond?'

'Oh, great, yeah,' Amy muttered. 'Absolutely fine…'

'All right,' said Reyn, slowly. 'I'll try to direct you through to the ship. I can't make any guarantees, but I'll try to get you through to the right time.' His ears pricked up. 'As for the dogs,' he pulled out a small golden device, 'I can put them on the wrong track for a while. Long enough for you to reach the ship.'

'Good man! Fox! Foxy-man-thing… Yes, whatever you are, you're good. Very good. We're good. Well, you do whatever it is you've got to do to confuse poor Inspector Galloway. While *Amy*,' he beckoned to her, 'why don't you come and help me choose which path to take?'

'I thought Reyn was going to guide you,' Amy said in a puzzled voice. 'Ow!' she finished, the Doctor having elbowed her hard. 'Yes! All right! I see! Yes! Let's choose an arch for you, Doctor! A really *nice* arch, one that looks like it's got Rory's name written all over it!'

They walked round the clearing and stopped by one of the arches of trees. It was winter over here, wet and gloomy. The Doctor made a big show of waving the sonic screwdriver about.

'I'd switch that on if I were you,' Amy said,

sotto voce. 'Looks more convincing that way.'

'Ah, yes.' The sonic started buzzing. 'Now, you've still got your triangulator, haven't you?'

'Of course!'

'Good. Always a good idea to have a back-up system.'

'Never noticed you worrying about that much before… Do you still not trust him?'

'Almost… But I think that war can do bad things to its victims, Amy. Reyn has been on his guard for a very long time. I doubt he's told us everything. So, no, I don't trust him, not entirely. Or, to be more accurate, I don't think he quite trusts me. Which means he might have some more surprises up his sleeve. Which means I'd like to make sure I have something up *my* sleeve. You know what to do if Rory's triangulator finally sends a signal?'

'I hit this button… no, *this* button. And then with any luck we'll all be able to find each other again without relying on Reyn, and I'll finally get my chocolatey treat. After which I'll brush and floss, naturally.'

'Excellent! Yes! Bang on! Chocolates and floss for all!'

'So… what was it you didn't want to say about the Long War?'

'Hmm?'

'You stopped yourself mid-sentence. What didn't you say?'

'Yes…' The Doctor sighed deeply. 'I know how that particular war ends, Amy, and it's a sad story. The thing is – I don't think Reyn realises that it's over. Done with.' He glanced back over his shoulder. 'Laura Brown's not the only one lost in time.'

'One last question, Doctor.'

'Make it quick.'

'You said before that going through one of these portals was irrevocable. But I've been through one, and I guess Rory must have been through one too, and you're about to go through one… Does that mean we're stuck here? Will we ever get out?'

Gently, he touched her cheek. 'Work to do first, Pond.'

'That's not an answer!'

'Of course it's an answer. If we want to get out, we'll have to make a way out.'

'Do you know how you're going to do that? No, no, I know the answer to that already. You're working on it.'

'How well you know me, Pond.' He smiled, and drew her in for a hug. 'Go back with Reyn. Guide me through to Rory. And watch out for any changes of heart at your end. Keep your finger on the button of the triangulator. And I promise you all the chocolate you want when we're done.'

'Actually it's the picnic I'm after now. Pork pie. Hey, watch out, I think Reyn's done.'

The Doctor switched off the sonic and patted the nearest tree. 'What a very fine pair of trees these are! These look just the trees for me! What do you think, Pond?'

'Oh, Doctor,' Amy said in delight, 'what a splendid pair of trees! If I had to choose some trees to take me back through time, these would be exactly the trees I'd choose!'

'Well, now that that's decided,' said the Doctor, 'how about we get on with it? Reyn, what about Inspector Galloway's search party?'

'It'll keep searching,' he said. 'But it won't find its way here. This whole area is now off limits, at least while the power holds. You should go now, Doctor. I can't hold them off indefinitely. Amy and I will return to my control room, and I'll guide you through to the ship.'

'No time like the present!' Standing framed by the arch of dark bare trees, the Doctor waved to Amy. 'Cheerio, Pond! See you later! Or earlier! But don't worry – I'll be ba—!'

The trees, and the Doctor, melted away.

In the courtyard of the castle, the rain was falling heavily. Laura greeted Amy and Reyn with great relief.

'Something's going wrong,' she said to Reyn. 'The whole place is breaking down.' She pointed up at the sky. 'Look!'

Amy looked up at a sky in confusion: patches of bright blue with fluffy white clouds here; sections of inky black spattered with stars there. It was as if parts thought it was day, and other parts were convinced it was night. A rainbow, broken into sections, was scattered haphazardly about.

'It's the Shift,' Amy told Laura. 'But we've found my friend, the Doctor. He thinks he can control the process, but first we have to guide him through to the ship. Reyn, this isn't looking good, really. We should hurry. What now?'

Reyn waved his hand in the familiar gesture. The whole castle disappeared, and the three of them were standing in a spherical room, with gun-metal walls. Steps led down to a console; Reyn ran down them and began operating controls.

Laura looked around her in amazement. 'I've never seen this place…'

'Breaks the illusion, doesn't it?' Amy followed Reyn down the steps. 'OK, are we in touch with the Doctor yet?'

'Not yet…' murmured Reyn, busy at the console. A high-pitched squeal filled the control room, making all three of them cover their ears. Then a voice came through.

'Pond! Pond! Doctor calling Pond! Can you hear me, Pond?'

'*Yes!*' Amy clenched her fists victoriously. 'Yes, I can hear you, you crazy time-travelling crazy thing! Where are you?'

'Where do you think I am, Pond? I'm in a wood, and it's raining. Why didn't we pack the umbrella?'

'Because we didn't want to look like Mary Poppins!'

'Ooh, fair point. How's it going at your end?'

'Oh, you know, the usual! End of things! Sky falling in!'

'Situation normal, then! Shan't worry about you too much! Reyn – which way now? We're aiming for 1917. Try not to land me in the middle of the Civil War. Or anywhere with dinosaurs. They're cool, but they're not very early twentieth century.'

As Reyn set about directing the Doctor through, Laura drew Amy aside.

'Amy, what does this all mean? Is everything

coming to an end?'

Amy, anxious to keep in touch with the Doctor, looked past her at the console. 'I don't know. The Doctor isn't there yet. And then we have to guide the ship through the Shift, and we still don't really know what's causing all the damage…' She glanced at Laura.

The old woman's face was wet with tears.

'Laura? Are you OK?'

'It's just that it's been such a very long time…' Laura whispered. 'Amy, did you meet my parents? Did you ever see them?'

Amy took hold of Laura's hand. Suddenly she realised the full extent of the old woman's predicament. Even if they guided the ship safely through the Shift, even if Reyn and the ship left without any damage to the woods and the town – it was all happening far too late for Laura. There was no bringing back the sixty years that she had been here.

'I wanted to travel,' Laura said. 'I wanted to see strange and beautiful places. And when I thought there was no way back, when I thought I could never see everyone and everywhere I loved again, it was easy to make myself believe that I had been somewhere wonderful, seen wonderful things. But now I'm not so certain any more. Amy, have I been deluding myself?

Have I been lost in a fantasy my whole life?'

'No,' Amy said, and held her hand tight. 'No, it's not been like that. What about Reyn? What about your friendship? An alien were-fox, Laura! That's pretty astounding! Try saying that at the school reunion! Who else do you know got to be friends with an alien?'

'You?' Laura said, and then she began to laugh. 'Yes,' she said, 'Yes, we've been friends. And you're right – not many people get to meet someone so extraordinary. Someone so unique.'

'It's not over till it's over, Laura. Nobody knows what ending they get, and happy endings are sometimes not what you've imagined. It looks like Reyn's going home. Perhaps you could go with him?'

Laura squeezed her hand. 'Perhaps.'

Reyn looked up from the console. His eyes were bright and his ears up and alert. 'Amy, I think we're nearly there. The Doctor's reached the ship.'

Amy and Laura hugged each other, and then rejoined Reyn at the console.

'Pond! Pond! Calling Pond! I'm here, Pond! I'm at the hatch into the ship! I'm going in! Any messages for Rory?'

Amy grabbed hold of the console. 'Give him

a kiss from me!'

'Doubt he'll let me, but I'll try my best! Opening the hatch now! Going in!'

There was a pause, the sound of the sonic screwdriver buzzing, and then an almighty *thump*. The room around Amy rocked alarmingly.

'Try not to finish us off when we're so close to success, Doctor,' Amy said. There was no reply. She leaned forwards anxiously. 'Doctor?'

Another thump.

'Ow... Yes! Yes! Still here! Everything's fine! It wasn't fine, and now it's fine again! Walking down a corridor... Some things never change... Here's a door... Shut door...' The sonic buzzed. *'Open door! Ooh, what – and who – do we have here?'*

In the background, Amy could hear voices, raised voices. 'Doctor! Are you OK? Is it Rory? Tell me it's Rory!'

The room around her shook again, and there was another brief squeal. Then the Doctor said, *'Hey! You two! Don't you know better than to quarrel in front of the children?'*

There was a pause, and then, to Amy's delight, Rory's voice came through – clear, annoyed, and extremely baffled.

'Who on earth *are you?'*

*

Lights dimming, some blacking out entirely, some turning red; an alarm going off – and now, standing at the top of the steps leading down to the console, there was a young man in a bow tie grinning down at Rory like a maniac.

This, Rory thought, really was the absolute limit.

'I don't know who you are,' he said hotly, 'but if you're the one behind all this, I want it stopped! I want it stopped now. I want my memories back, and I want to go home. Wherever that is. Which I don't know. Because *somebody* has got their spaceship to pinch my memories! Well, I'm telling you,' he raised his finger, not too high, he didn't want cause too much trouble, just to get his point across, 'it's not good enough!'

Bow-tie man beamed at him and then swung down the stairs. He bounded over to Rory and planted a kiss on the top of his head. Rory pushed him away.

'No! Stop! Get off! This isn't fair!'

'*Rory?*' A young woman's voice echoed through the control room, piercing through the whine of the alarm. '*What time do you call this!*'

'Oh, Mr Amy Pond,' said bow-tie man, shaking his head. 'You've stayed out too late, and the wife isn't happy.'

Emily, kneeling beside Harry, couldn't quite suppress a chuckle. Bow-tie man swung round and favoured her with another lunatic smile. 'Miss Emily Bostock!' he said. 'At last! What an *absolute* pleasure to meet you!'

'Oh!' said Emily, nicely. 'Lovely to meet you too, sir!' Bow-tie man went over to join her, and Rory, bewildered, followed. Kneeling down beside Emily, the new arrival took hold of Harry's other hand.

'Well,' he said, calmly. 'I bet you're frightened! That's all right. World's a strange place, isn't it? Confusing. You're not sure what to think and you're not sure what to do. I'm the Doctor, by the way. I'm here to help.'

The Doctor... Rory rubbed his forehead. Lights dimmed and reddened around him. The alarm was very distracting.

'It found out, you see,' Emily said to the Doctor. 'About all the people that it brought here. And it got terribly upset. I think that's what's making everything shake about.'

Harry trembled and the walls of the ship rocked. The whine went up a notch.

'Oh, please, love!' Emily cried softly. 'Don't! Don't!'

'*Stolen...*' whispered the ship through Harry. '*Sorry... Sorry to be born...*'

'Yes, I see,' said the Doctor softly. 'Thought about someone else for the first time. Scary when that happens. Thought about what it had done to them. Even scarier.' He rubbed Harry's hand. 'Emily, ever helped anyone give birth before?'

'Well,' Emily said doubtfully, 'the *pigs*...'

'Er, excuse me!' Rory tapped the Doctor on the shoulder. 'What exactly is going on here?'

'Rory, yes! Sorry! Memory loss! Haven't forgotten – how ironic would that be? I'm onto it! But right now we've got to deal with the ship. You probably noticed – what with the alarms and the lights and everything – that something's going on. Well, that something is called its Shift, which means it's coming alive, and I think all this talk about its terrible evildoing hasn't exactly helped—'

'But it's true! It's stolen people! Taken them away and used them!'

Harry – the whole ship – convulsed once again at his words. More patches along the walls went dark and the howling alarm screamed louder, like the ship was in pain.

'Rory,' said the Doctor, 'you need to shut up. *Now.*'

'But it's only a ship. I—!'

'*Rory!*' Again, the young woman's voice rang

round the room. '*Button it!*'

Rory, as if programmed to, obeyed. He clamped his mouth shut and froze.

'*End...*' moaned the ship through Harry's lips. '*Finish... The only way...*'

'Now wherever are you getting that idea?' said the Doctor briskly. 'All right, so it's not nice to go about dragging people off and stealing their memories, but nobody told you not to, and as soon as you realised, you stopped. Can't say fairer than that, can you? What's all this about finishing yourself? That's a terrible idea!'

'*Scared... ran away... Shouldn't have... Don't want it... Don't want to be me...*'

'Oh Harry!' exclaimed Emily. 'Nobody thinks that! Nobody blames you! Anyone who does is wicked or a fool!'

'*Sacrifice... like the others... there has to be a sacrifice...*'

'Oh, an even worse idea!' said the Doctor. 'Where are you picking these things up from? Who are you hanging round with? Emily, who exactly is Harry?'

'My friend. He ran away into the woods rather than get called up. Ship took him. This is his body.'

'Oh... Oh, I see! So Harry's are some of the most recent memories Ship's got to draw on.

And Ship's confused its own guilt about the disappearances with Harry's shame about deserting...'

'And Ship's got the idea that to make amends there has to be a sacrifice,' Emily said. 'Oh, Harry, you poor thing! Who wants you out there in all that murder? Who in their right mind would want that? Not me, love!' She started to cry. 'Don't give up, dear! Stay with me! I can't lose another, not after Sammy...'

'Ship,' the Doctor urged, 'you've got access to other memories, haven't you? Other people came here too, didn't they? Not just Harry. So what about them? What do you know from them? What can they tell you?' He looked back over his shoulder to where Rory was standing by, silent and befuddled.

'What about Mr Amy Pond?' said the Doctor. 'Trooper Rory Williams? What about his memories? Can you see him, Ship, standing guard over the woman he loves, for two thousand years? What an amazing sacrifice! And nobody – absolutely nobody – had to die!'

As he spoke a light switched on in Rory's head. 'Er,' he said, 'actually, that wasn't me...'

'No. It wasn't,' said the Doctor. (And of course this was the Doctor! How did you forget the *Doctor…*?) 'Not technically. But it was you in all the ways that matter. You'd do it if you had to, Rory Williams. Plastic or not, you'd find a way to stand guard for ever if you had to.'

And Rory knew he would – for Amy. His amazing, wonderful, alarming, smashing Amy, the memory of whom flooded back into his head now. Rory nearly cried to think he could ever have forgotten her.

'Amy!' he called out. 'I'm not in trouble, am I?'

'*No, you're not in trouble!*' A pause. '*Well, not today.*'

The alarm sounded mournfully. '*End…*' said the ship-through-Harry. '*Die…*'

'Oh, love!' Emily said. 'I don't want you to die! Nor Harry, neither! There's been enough of that. Please, Ship! Listen to us! Nobody wants you to die!'

Rory, understanding fully now what was happening, rested his hands on Emily's shoulder. 'Ship,' he said urgently. 'Emily's right. You made a mistake, that's all. You're sorry, and you've stopped. That's enough. You don't need to do any more.'

For a moment, there was only the sound of the alarm, howling, the ship's guilt and shame and sorrow. Then: '*Not consistent… Rory… Why not consistent?'*

'I was wrong,' Rory said simply. 'I changed my mind. But that's OK. You don't always have to be right. You're allowed to change your mind. You should, if you're wrong. That's what being a person is about.'

'Not… consistent…'

The walls shook violently. Rory had to grab onto the console to stay upright. Harry was flung forwards, sending Emily crashing to the floor beneath him. The ship's wail reached its crescendo. Then it, and the lights, cut out. It felt to Rory as if he had been picked up, shaken hard, and then dumped down again slightly to one side.

For a moment, everything was dark and silent. Then the lights, yellow and green, slowly lifted. There was a brief further moment of silence, and then the ship spoke, but not through Harry. Now its voice came from all around.

'I understand,' said Ship, calmly. 'Shift is achieved. Situation stable.'

Harry blinked and his eyes went back to their usual blue. He looked down at Emily, lying in a heap under him. 'Emmy?' he said. 'What the devil's going on?'

Emily laughed in delight.

'Congratulations,' the Doctor announced

proudly to all listening. 'It's a beautiful baby ship.'

Back in Reyn's control room, Amy punched the air.

'Yes! Oh, Doctor, you're amazing! And as for you, Rory Williams...' She blew him a kiss. 'You're adorable!'

She felt Laura's hand suddenly grip her arm.

'Amy...' the old woman whispered.

Amy turned around. Reyn, from somewhere, had produced a weapon, a large weapon, the kind that alien foxes might use to fight their enemies.

'Ship,' Reyn called out. 'This is your captain speaking. Prepare to report for duty.' He looked sadly at the two women. 'Laura, Amy – I'm sorry. But Ship and I have our duty to perform. We have to return to the War.'

Chapter
13

'Oh no you bloomin' well don't!' Emily Bostock shouted back at the disembodied voice echoing around her. She gripped onto Harry's arm like a tigress making ready to defend her cubs. 'Whoever you might be, you just think on! No one here is going to the War. Not Ship, not Harry, not anyone! Over my dead body!'

'Got to hope it won't come to that, Emily,' the Doctor said softly, and then addressed Reyn. 'Reyn, I don't much like the sound of this. Sounds – I don't know, a bit too much like bossing someone about. Why don't we ask Ship what it wants to do now?'

'*Doctor,*' said Reyn, '*I'm grateful for all that you have done for me. But this is no longer your concern. It's not a question of what Ship wants to do. It's a question of duty. Ship knows what's required of it, and so do I. It's been a long war for all of us, Doctor, but it's not over yet.'*

'Ship,' said the Doctor. 'Is that what you want? To go back to the War?'

'You don't have to, Ship, love!' Emily said fiercely. 'Not if you don't want to! It's a waste! A terrible, wicked waste!'

The Doctor touched her arm. 'Let Ship decide, Emily,' he said quietly. 'Ship can do whatever it wants.'

Rory watched as, on the console, images sped past of all the people that Ship had gathered over the centuries.

Eventually, Reyn's voice came through again. He was getting impatient. *'Ship. It's your duty—'*

'No,' said Ship evenly. 'I disagree. I shall not go.'

'That's desertion, Ship. Mutiny. I can take action—'

'I shall not go,' Ship said again.

'Sounds like Ship's made up its mind, Reyn,' the Doctor said. 'So why don't we come up with another plan—'

He stopped speaking when the air on the far side of the console began to fill with particles of golden light. Quickening, solidifying, the shimmering space resolved itself into Reyn, Laura, and Amy. Amy gave Rory a little wave.

'Hi, gorgeous,' she said. 'Love to come and give you a "hello" kiss. But look: there's a weapon-wielding were-fox in the way.'

Rory gave her an anxious little wave back. The return of his memories definitely had both good and bad aspects. Good – Amy. Bad – he was the kind of person who could get separated from his loved one by big alien guns carried by humanoid foxes.

Reyn gestured to the Doctor and the others. 'Over here, please,' he said, backing round the console, his weapon covering them all. Bright lights flashed on the console and a voice began to chant. It sounded very much like a countdown.

'What's he doing?' demanded Emily. 'Here, what are you doing?'

'I'd like to know too, please, Reyn,' said the Doctor.

Reyn's free hand moved quickly around the console. 'If Ship's mind is made up, then Ship's mind must be made to change.' The hand upon the weapon shook. 'The Shift is only newly completed. I can still undo it. Ship's sentience can be reversed.'

'That's obscene!' Amy said. 'Ship's alive now!

You'd be cutting out its mind! That's murder!'

'Worse than murder,' the Doctor said. 'The shell of the ship would be intact. It would fly – but it would no longer think.'

'I'm within my rights,' Reyn said defensively. 'Summary execution is the penalty for desertion—'

'You... *monster*!' Emily cried. 'Doctor, have at him!'

'Everyone, calm down,' the Doctor said. 'Reyn, I don't believe that you want to do this.'

'I have to get back! They're dying, Doctor! You said you knew about our war! You should understand!'

'I know. I know that what happened to your world – to your people – was a terrible crime. And so is this!' He took a step forwards, but Reyn lifted the weapon again. 'Reyn, Ship is bound up with this place, entangled with it. If you destroy Ship's mind – what effect will that have on the people around here? Everybody has been affected by Ship's growing consciousness! And now that the Shift has happened... What would that do to them, Reyn? Have you thought about that?'

Again, Reyn wavered. The weapon slipped down slightly and his hand hovered above the console. Then he shook himself, and straightened up, military-style, except that the uniform didn't quite seem to fit. 'No. They're dying in hundreds of thousands back home, Doctor. I can still make a difference.'

'Reyn,' Laura pleaded softly. 'Please don't do this. My parents – they're out there! I've talked to you about them, many times. All the years we spent together. All that we've seen together. Please don't do this!'

'Laura, dear lady!' Reyn's sad orange eyes were bright and wet. There was something desperate about him. 'It's a risk I have to take.'

The voice was still chanting down.

'Doctor!' Amy said. 'Stop him!'

'All right,' the Doctor said. 'Pond! Mr Pond! Both of you! Triangulate!'

Amy and Rory looked at each other, pulled out their twin devices, pressed the long-unpressed buttons…

And with a groan and a sigh, as if remarking to anyone listening that perhaps it was getting rather old for this game, the TARDIS materialised at the top of the stairs.

The uninitiated gawked at her. 'What the devil is *that*?' said Harry.

The Doctor beamed up at it. 'My ship! Isn't she cool?'

Emily sniffed. 'Bit small.'

'So far I've liked you, Emily Bostock. Let's not quarrel now.' The Doctor swung round to face Reyn. 'Now. You. Here's the deal. Gorgeous blue box up there – travels through time and space. She's nifty! So.' He pointed at Reyn. 'You leave Ship alone.' He pointed at himself. 'I take you back home.' He waved his hands around. 'Ship stays here because you no longer need it for the journey. Everyone happy. How does that sound?'

'But Ship is an important part of our arsenal,' Reyn said doubtfully. 'We're fighting a losing battle. We need everything—'

'Reyn,' the Doctor said, 'you may be a soldier now, but you're not a murderer. If you truly cared so little for life, you would have left this planet centuries ago! But you did the right thing! You were prepared to sacrifice yourself to protect the people of this town. Don't waste that sacrifice, Reyn, all those long years you spent here. Let me take you back. Leave Ship here. We can take care of it.'

Reyn lowered his head. His ears went flat.

'It's the right thing to do,' Laura said.

The gun went down.

'All right,' Reyn said. 'All right, Doctor – I'll trust you. Take me home.'

*

Leaving Amy in charge on board Ship, the Doctor took Rory and Reyn into the TARDIS. He waved his hands around.

'Isn't she gorgeous? I mean, I know Ship is a very impressive piece of temporal-spatial engineering, Reyn, but I think the TARDIS's take on the whole business is so much more elegant… and none of that accidentally turning a nearby piece of woodland into a trap for passing strangers—'

'Doctor,' said Reyn wearily. 'You were taking me home.'

'So I was! Home! Home time for Reyn!' The Doctor clapped his hands together, and then did the series of random moves and leaps around the console that Rory had come to recognise meant that a journey in time and space was under way.

'Home?' said the Doctor. 'I can get you back home to your foxy-man world in as much time as it takes to say foxy-man world inhabitant…' He yanked the control that landed the TARDIS, opened the door, pointed outside, and said, 'There you are, Reyn. Recognise it yet?'

Reyn walked slowly outside, the gun hanging limply from his hand. Rory, following him out, stepped onto a world that looked like it might be the kind of place inhabited by alien foxes.

The air was spicy. Sharp angled buildings sunk underground into deep tunnels lit with golden lights. Turrets spiked high into the clouds, silhouetted against an orange sun.

'This looks like home,' Reyn said, slowly, 'but not how I remember it.' He shook his head. 'Have I been gone so long?'

'You've been gone longer than you imagine,' the Doctor said quietly. 'This *is* your home, Reyn, but not when you knew it. This is what your home is going to be. After the Long War. Long, long after.'

Reyn stared around, bewildered by this half-familiar world. 'I don't understand,' he said. 'The War's *over*? Who won?'

'Nobody won,' the Doctor said. 'Nobody wins at war. But your species survived, if that's what you mean. They were conquered first –'

Reyn shuddered.

'– and they suffered for a long time, a very long time. Then the empire that conquered them declined, as empires do, in the end, and your people became free again. They weren't like they were before – no, how could they be, after all that? They changed. Became a little harder, a little more mistrustful, a little disenchanted. They'd lost a great deal. But they survived. They went on. And that world, down there – thousands of years have passed since your war. The Long War's hardly even history to them – it's more the stuff of legend. Like Troy and Hector are to Rory. Like Achilles and Cassandra and… um, Sherlock Holmes.'

'Doctor,' Rory whispered, 'Sherlock Holmes wasn't real…'

'Oh, yes, people *say* that…' The Doctor went on: 'Reyn, here, in this time, you're the stuff of legend too! They tell stories about you – the lost traveller. They talk about how one day you'll return, and you'll bring with you the knowledge, the way to teach ships to think and speak and be. They don't know how to do that on your world now. They forgot after the Long War.'

'Doctor,' Rory whispered again, 'is that all true?'

'It will be,' the Doctor whispered back, 'soon enough.' To Reyn, he said, 'You spent a long time in the woods, Reyn. Longer than you realised. But time didn't stand still out here. Your war is long since over. But your world is still here, and it's been waiting for you to return. The lost traveller has come home.'

Reyn's shoulders had slumped. His head was down and his ears low. Slowly he turned to look at the Doctor.

'Home? How can this place be home? Everyone I knew and loved is gone! Oh, Doctor!' His voice was full of grief. 'Why have you brought me here? I would rather have died with everyone I knew and loved than be lost like this!' His orange eyes, clever and sad, looked back at the TARDIS. And then he said, 'You said this machine could travel in time. You could take me back! Take me back home! Take me back to where I belong!'

His hand tightened around his gun. Rory whispered, 'Doctor…?'

And then someone called out. 'The traveller! It is, isn't it! Look! The traveller!'

A child, or someone who easily remembered being a child, red-furred and long-muzzled and bright-eyed. 'Look! It *is* him, isn't it!' He called over to his friends. 'Come and look at this! Look at the uniform, the plasma gun – it's like something from a history book! He's even got the scar on his nose! It is! It's the *Traveller*!'

Others passing paused to look too, and their faces changed the moment they caught sight of Reyn. As Rory watched, a crowd quickly formed around the lost old pilot, people whose sheer foxiness was almost overwhelming. They gathered round, chattering, reaching out to touch Reyn, and, suddenly, he was lifted high up, and the air was filled with laughter and delight. Some songs remain the same.

The Doctor looked out at the scene. He was smiling. 'It's been a long time since Reyn breathed his own air or held hands that are the same as his. But he's home now, Rory, and he's welcome here. It's time for us to go.'

And so, very quietly, they slipped away.

'Back to Ship, I suppose,' said Rory, as the TARDIS doors closed behind them. 'What is it we have to do there?'

'Well, we still have to release Ship from all that human history in which it's entangled itself and then send it on its way. Back to the stars. Back to exploring and learning and knowing... Ooh, though,' the Doctor twiddled some dials and yanked some levers, 'one last job to do around here before we leave local space...'

Patiently, the TARDIS landed again in the same place.

'Where are we now?' said Rory. 'And when?'

'Same where,' replied the Doctor, 'but quite a lot earlier when it comes to when. I said that Reyn was a legend, Rory – the lost traveller – and that's all true, or rather, it will be, once we've had a chance to fiddle the books.'

'Fiddle the books?' Rory looked at him in

horror. 'What are you getting me into now?'

'I mean the history books!'

'Oh, well, if you only meant fiddle the history books I suppose that's fine!'

'Legends don't come from nowhere, you know! Somebody has to... legendate... legendify... Make it all up in the first place! The story needs to be seeded, about the lost traveller from the Long War, who returns with the forgotten knowledge of his age, how to build the famous living ships... So we need to have a few words in some foxy ears from the past, get them twitching, get a few stories started... Just set the whole thing going so the legends are written down by the time Reyn arrives. You know the kind of thing: *And, lo, it was promised that the traveller would return, and we would know him from the great blue box that came from nowhere, heralding his homecoming...*' The Doctor frowned. 'Actually, probably quickest if I just write them down myself. Pass me that biro, will you?'

Amy watched with relief as the TARDIS rematerialised on board Ship. Out came the Doctor, Rory at his heels.

'Sorted?' Amy said.

'Of course!'

'So where is Reyn?' asked Laura anxiously.

'Is he safe? Is he happy?'

'Yes, he's safe – and soon I think he'll realise that he's happy. He's back amongst his own people now. He's a legend. A living legend. I think he'll soon be happier than he's ever been.' He smiled at Laura. 'And now… Well. Laura Brown. I think you know what has to happen next.'

Amy glanced suspiciously at the regretful looks Laura and the Doctor were giving each other. 'What? Doctor, what else have you got up your sleeve? And why do I think I won't like it?'

'We guided Ship through its Shift, Amy, and we saw Reyn safely on his way. But Ship is still here, still bound up with Swallow Woods, and it can still affect Foxton and the people that live there. All those time pockets and spatial wotsits, they're scattered around Swallow Woods like leaves, waiting to pull people in, sending them through the portal place. But we can fix it.'

'Er, getting lost now, Doctor,' Rory said. 'How do we fix it?'

'Laura knows, I think.'

'Laura?' said Amy. She turned to the old woman. 'What? What do you know?'

'I think,' Laura said slowly, 'that I have to stay here. Or, rather, stay in the environment that Reyn created. To seal it from behind. Close up time around me… Because everything that's happened to me here – that can't be taken back. I went into Swallow Woods, and I met Reyn – and Ship – and I spent sixty years here with them. None of that can be taken back, or it will undo the Doctor's fix, too. But that will be the end of it. Am I right, Doctor?'

'Nearly,' the Doctor said. 'But not quite. You're right that we can't take back what's happened to you, Laura. You're the last, now that Vicky and Jess are home. But Ship doesn't have to be here throughout all of time. We can send Ship on its way now… Well, one specific now. Your now. It will have to have been here for you to visit. And for Emily and Harry too. But not before. Or in between. Or since.'

'Wait,' said Amy. 'Let me make sure I've got this straight. If we want to rid Swallow Woods of Ship's influence, we can – but Laura *has* to have come here and spent all that time here. Laura's timeline can't be reversed.'

'And why would I want my life reversed? Would you? Would anyone?' Laura bristled.

'It isn't so much about reversing. Time's not like that. It's more… fluid. But no, Laura, no one is going to change your story-so-far,' said the Doctor. 'Although, where it goes now is up to you. The world that you shared with Reyn will disappear when Ship sets out – but I don't think Ship would mind some company for the road.'

Ship's walls shimmered in a gentle confirmation.

'But your parents!' Amy said in dismay. 'Your family!'

'If I go back,' Laura said, 'I'll be older than my parents, much older! How do we explain that? And you know how I wanted to travel, Amy. How I wanted to see new things… And I will! This time, I really will!'

'And you're only going into space!' the Doctor said. 'That's no reason not to stay in touch!'

'Doctor,' said Emily worriedly. 'What about us? Me and Harry. We're part of it. We've come this way, too, haven't we?'

'Well, Miss Emily Bostock – that's entirely up to you. Laura, really, is the one that matters. Laura's the one that *has* to take this path. You can go home, Emily. And you, Harry.'

'But we don't have to go home, do we? We could leave, too?' said Emily. 'There's nothing stopping us from going with them?'

'Not at all! Ship has been here in your time to meet you. So no, there's nothing stopping you going with them, Emily. If you want.'

'Then I'll go,' she said, and turned to Laura. 'If you don't mind, missus. If you don't mind some company?'

Laura laughed. 'Of course I don't mind!'

Emily turned to Harry and held out her hand. 'What do you say, love? Won't you come too?'

'Away?' Harry said. He looked around uncertainly. 'You sure it's safe, Emmy?'

'Safe,' said the Doctor helpfully, 'is a matter of perspective. But it's probably better than 1917.'

'Which,' Rory muttered, 'you told me was absolutely nothing to worry about.'

'Ah. Yes. Mostly. *Mostly* nothing to worry about. But I'd say heading into space on board a living ship probably beats 1917. And certainly beats the trenches.'

That was enough to convince Harry.

'Live and learn,' the Doctor said. 'Good choice.'

The travellers watched as, on the TARDIS screen, Swallow Woods released Ship from its embrace. The trees rocked and parted, and the living ship lifted from the ground and then left, taking its new crew to the stars. A few golden trails spun wildly in its wake, and then drifted away. For one brief second, Amy thought she glimpsed a huge fantastic castle with a rainbow overhead – but the vision slipped away before she could even be certain it was there.

'What about all the other people, Doctor?' Amy said. She started to pin Emily's butterfly brooch back onto her jacket. Emily had told her to keep it, to remember her by. 'The other ones that went missing that we never even met? The ones that were only marks in books?'

Suddenly, Rory's hands took charge of the brooch. He pinned it in place, and then kissed Amy gently on the tip of her nose.

'You're great.'

'So are you.'

'I missed you.'

'I missed you too.'

'So…' said the Doctor, spinning round on his heels. 'Well… Yes… The other people. Good question, Pond. Of course, Ship and Reyn never visited all those times, now. So they never disappeared. There was no Ship to take them on board, no Reyn to direct them to his fantasy world – they'll just walk through Swallow Woods.'

'Not Emily, though,' Rory said. 'Or Harry.'

'No, they've met Ship, and they've left with Ship. They will have disappeared, and without explanation. I suppose people will most likely say that Harry's run away rather than get called up… But what about Emily? What will they say about her? The last anyone saw of Emily Bostock, she was leaving the pub with a strange young man…'

'Oh…!' said Amy, rounding on Rory with an evil glimmer in her eye. 'I can just imagine the story! Emily Bostock, last seen heading into the woods, tempted away by a handsome stranger!'

'Well that's just *great*, isn't it?' said Rory, as Amy wrapped her arms around him. 'Now the history books have me down as some sort of *rake*…!'

Amy shook her head. 'Nah! Not very likely, is it? Besides, you're mine. But they all make it through, Doctor? They don't get lost?'

'Come and see,' the Doctor said.

He pushed open the TARDIS doors. Below them lay Swallow Woods and the land around, which they had come to know so well over the past few days. 'Looks exactly like one of those aerial photographs,' Amy said. 'Poor Jess. They nearly frightened the life out of her.'

'Watch,' the Doctor said.

And as Amy and Rory watched, the landscape beneath them began to alter, like a piece of film being speeded up. They watched the seasons pass over Swallow Woods, watched the trees spring to life and fall away again in winter. They saw people walk along the path that led into the woods – and they saw them all come out again.

'That's wonderful,' Rory said softly. 'All going home.'

'Oh yes, very nice,' said Amy, and, when Rory and the Doctor turned to stare at her, added, 'I do mean it! But I was promised chocolate. And a picnic. And pie.'

And what now, for the people of Foxton? Where does time, unravelling back and flowing forwards, take them? What now, for Swallow Woods?

Gordon Galloway, sitting in traffic on the motorway between Junctions 11 and 12, ponders the three impossible things that happened to him before breakfast. First of all, the nightmare – a terrible nightmare, of being trapped in a forest, in the middle of a storm, running in circles and unable to escape, while dogs howled miserably around him. A nightmare so real that when the alarm woke him, he was sweating, and sure that his hair would be soaked with rain and his clothes filthy from mud and leaves.

But, no. He'd been tucked up safe and warm in bed, and, beyond the bedroom window, the rain had stopped, and a damp bright autumn dawn unfolded as he watched.

That had only been the start. On his way downstairs, the phone rang. A terrible line, as if someone was calling long distance. He could barely make out the speaker's voice at first.

'Inspector Galloway? We've not spoken before, but my name is Laura Brown.'

'Laura! My God, girl, are you all right? Where have you *been*?'

'I'm fine, I'm fine, don't worry! I know I've caused a lot of trouble and I'm sorry. The truth is, I got into a terrible tizzy about my exams, and I decided to start my gap year early—'

'Where *are* you? There's been a search... the papers got hold of it... We've all been terrified for you!'

'I know, and I'm sorry. I'm... about to board a flight. Now don't make a fuss! I've spoken to my parents and it's all just fine. I'm going to be travelling for a while. It's what I wanted to do, what I really wanted to do, not exams. Maybe I'll do them some other time. I've got to go now, Inspector! They're calling me to... to the gate. I'm on my way! At last! Goodbye, Mr Galloway, goodbye! Thank you for worrying so much about me! Everything's fine! You

don't have to worry any more!'

And she'd hung up, leaving him standing there like a small boy who'd been told what's what by his old granny. It was bewildering. Had she always been so self-assured? He rang her parents at once, of course. Tearfully, they told him what he was desperate to hear: that they had spoken to Laura too, and that she was safe. And that was what counted, he supposed…

The morning hadn't quite finished with him yet. Last of all, but still before his first sip of tea had been given the chance to touch his lips, Mary, his beloved wife, put down her own cup and said: 'Sweetheart, I've been thinking. Why don't we move back north?'

The traffic inched forwards. Gordon Galloway counted his blessings.

On the high street that morning, Vicky Caine, on her way to school, popped into the florists to send her mum an apology for missing the last bus and (heinous crime) walking home.

Across the road, Ruby Porter stopped at the newsagents to buy a birthday card for her favourite uncle, Peter, who was 67 later in the week. Then she hopped into her little blue car and drove to the college in the next town, where she lectured in history. She was looking forward to her day. She wasn't facing any disciplinary action. She had never joined the police.

Outside Foxton's ordinary police station, the people from the papers and the television channels, briefed now about the safe return of Laura Brown, were packing up and heading back to the city. Inside, in an ordinary interview room, a clock mended itself while the blind remained broken. And down the road, in the parish church, the records quietly tidied themselves, a number of curious green marks disappearing for good.

Jess Ashcroft stood on Long Lane by a signpost watching a big blue police box dematerialise. In her head, she still held two sets of memories. One set of memories was alarming and amazing and astonishing – and they were slowly fading away, becoming dreamier, replaced by another story: the sudden disappearance of Laura Brown, the brief flurry of press interest, and then Laura's reappearance online. Soon that would be all that remained.

The TARDIS was gone. Jess climbed over the fence and walked down the hill to Swallow Woods. There was a path across the field that forked: one way went to the road, the other led under the trees deep into the woods. Jess took this path. She knew the way very well. She'd come here a lot as a child, despite parental warnings. You couldn't keep kids away from Swallow Woods. It was their playground.

The path brought her in time to a clearing in the heart of the woods, where a deep old pool lay amidst a temple of trees. Jess sat beneath an old oak magnificent with autumn colour. The blue box (not to mention its strange and alarming inhabitants) had now slipped her mind…

Jess takes out her phone and balances it between her hands, wondering what to do next. Yesterday, at the press conference, she'd told a journalist from a national paper that Laura Brown would turn up today. This morning, as he was packing up, he'd waved her over and given her his phone number. So what should she do? Stay in the town she knows so well, better than anyone, probably, or leave, go on, go elsewhere, somewhere new…?

Her phone beeps. A message from Lily.

Hey LOIS (Lily had written) *did you see Luara's facebook update: she sez 'Laura Brown is reaching for the stars.'*

Jess puts away her phone and takes out a coin. Heads, she goes; tails, she stays. She throws the coin up into the air, where it hangs for a split second, silvery bright in a shaft of sunshine, full of potential, and then falls to the ground...

Acknowledgements

With grateful thanks to Justin Richards, Gary Russell, Steve Tribe, and Kat Woods. Love and thanks as ever to Matthew.

And thanks to Fairport Convention for recording 'Reynardine'.

Available now from BBC Books:

DOCTOR WHO
Nuclear Time
by Oli Smith

£6.99 ISBN 978 1 846 07989 4

Colorado, 1981. The Doctor, Amy and Rory arrive in Appletown – an idyllic village in the remote American desert where the townsfolk go peacefully about their suburban routines. But when two more strangers arrive, things begin to change.

The first is a mad scientist – whose warnings are cut short by an untimely and brutal death. The second is the Doctor…

As death falls from the sky, the Doctor is trapped. The TARDIS is damaged, and the Doctor finds he is living backwards through time. With Amy and Rory being hunted through the suburban streets of the Doctor's own future and getting farther away with every passing second, he must unravel the secrets of Appletown before time runs out…

A thrilling, all-new adventure featuring the Doctor, Amy and Rory, as played by Matt Smith, Karen Gillan and Arthur Darvill in the spectacular hit series from BBC Television.

Available now from BBC Books:

DOCTOR ⏣ WHO
The King's Dragon
by Una McCormack

£6.99 ISBN 978 1 846 07990 0

In the city-state of Geath, the King lives in a golden hall, and the people want for nothing. Everyone is happy and everyone is rich. Or so it seems.

When the Doctor, Amy and Rory look beneath the surface, they discover a city of secrets. In dark corners, strange creatures are stirring. At the heart of the hall, a great metal dragon oozes gold. Then the Herald appears, demanding the return of her treasure... And next come the gunships.

The battle for possession of the treasure has begun, and only the Doctor and his friends can save the people of the city from being destroyed in the crossfire of an ancient civil war. But will the King surrender his new-found wealth? Or will he fight to keep it...?

A thrilling, all-new adventure featuring the Doctor, Amy and Rory, as played by Matt Smith, Karen Gillan and Arthur Darvill in the spectacular hit series from BBC Television.

Available now from BBC Books:

DOCTOR ☐ WHO

The Glamour Chase

by Gary Russell

£6.99 ISBN 978 1 846 07988 7

An archaeological dig in 1936 unearths relics of another time… And – as the Doctor, Amy and Rory realise – another place. Another planet.

But if Enola Porter, noted adventuress, has really found evidence of an alien civilisation, how come she isn't famous? Why has Rory never heard of her? Added to that, since Amy's been travelling with him for a while now, why does she now think the Doctor is from Mars?

As the ancient spaceship reactivates, the Doctor discovers that nothing and no one can be trusted. The things that seem most real could actually be literal fabrications – and very deadly indeed.

Who can the Doctor believe when no one is what they seem? And how can he defeat an enemy who can bend matter itself to their will? For the Doctor, Amy and Rory – and all of humanity – the buried secrets of the past are very much a threat to the present...

A thrilling, all-new adventure featuring the Doctor, Amy and Rory, as played by Matt Smith, Karen Gillan and Arthur Darvill in the spectacular hit series from BBC Television.

DOCTOR ⬚ WHO
The Only Good Dalek

by Justin Richards and Mike Collins

£12.99 ISBN 978 1 846 07984 9

Station 7 is where the Earth Forces send all the equipment captured in their unceasing war against the Daleks. It's where Dalek technology is analysed and examined. It's where the Doctor and Amy have just arrived. But somehow the Daleks have found out about Station 7 – and there's something there that they want back.

With the Doctor increasingly worried about the direction the Station's research is taking, the commander of Station 7 knows he has only one possible, desperate, defence. Because the last terrible secret of Station 7 is that they don't only store captured Dalek technology. It's also a prison. And the only thing that might stop a Dalek is another Dalek…

An epic, full-colour graphic novel featuring the Doctor and Amy, as played by Matt Smith and Karen Gillan in the spectacular hit series from BBC Television.

DOCTOR WHO

The Coming of the Terraphiles

by Michael Moorcock

£16.99 ISBN 978 1 846 07983 2

Miggea – a star on the very edge of reality. The cusp between this universe and the next. A point where space-time has worn thin, and is in danger of collapsing… And the venue for the grand finals of the competition to win the fabled Arrow of Law.

The Doctor and Amy have joined the Terraphiles – a group dedicated to re-enacting ancient sporting events. They are determined to win the Arrow. But just getting to Miggea proves tricky. Reality is collapsing, ships are disappearing, and Captain Cornelius and his pirates are looking for easy pickings.

Even when they arrive, the Doctor and Amy's troubles won't be over. They have to find out who is so desperate to get the Arrow of Law that they will kill for it. And uncover the traitor on their own team. And win the contest fair and square.

And, of course, they need to save the universe from total destruction.

A thrilling, all-new adventure featuring the Doctor and Amy, as played by Matt Smith and Karen Gillan in the spectacular hit series from BBC Television, written by the acclaimed science fiction and fantasy author Michael Moorcock.

DOCTOR ▢ WHO
Dead of Winter

by James Goss

£6.99 ISBN 978 1 849 90238 0

In Dr Bloom's clinic at a remote spot on the Italian coast, at the end of the eighteenth century, nothing is ever quite what it seems.

Maria is a lonely little girl with no one to play with. She writes letters to her mother from the isolated resort where she is staying. She tells of the pale English aristocrats and the mysterious Russian nobles and their attentive servants. She tells of intrigue and secrets, and she tells of strange faceless figures that rise from the sea. She writes about the enigmatic Mrs Pond who arrives with her husband and her physician, and who will change everything.

What she doesn't tell her mother is the truth that everyone knows and no one says – that the only people who come here do so to die...

A thrilling, all-new adventure featuring the Doctor, Amy and Rory, as played by Matt Smith, Karen Gillan and Arthur Darvill in the spectacular hit series from BBC Television.

Available now from BBC Books:

DOCTOR ⬚ WHO
Hunter's Moon
by Paul Finch

£6.99 ISBN 978 1 849 90236 6

Welcome to Leisure Platform 9 – a place where gamblers and villains rub shoulders with socialites and celebrities. Don't cheat at the games tables, and be careful who you beat. The prize for winning the wrong game is to take part in another, as Rory is about to discover – and the next game could be the death of him.

When Rory is kidnapped by the brutal crime lord Xord Krauzzen, the Doctor and Amy must go undercover to infiltrate the deadly contest being played out in the ruins of Gorgoror. But how long before Krauzzen realises the Doctor isn't a vicious mercenary and discovers what Amy is up to? It's only a matter of time.

And time is the one thing Rory and the other fugitives on Gorgoror don't have. They are the hunted in a game that can only end in death, and time for everyone is running out…

A thrilling, all-new adventure featuring the Doctor, Amy and Rory, as played by Matt Smith, Karen Gillan and Arthur Darvill in the spectacular hit series from BBC Television.

Coming soon from BBC Books:

DOCTOR WHO
Paradox Lost

by George Mann

£6.99 ISBN 978 1 849 90235 9

London 1910: An unsuspecting thief gets more than he bargained for when he breaks into a house in Kensington. He finds himself confronted by horrific, grey-skinned creatures that are waiting to devour his mind.

London 3189: An unimaginably ancient city. The remains of an android are dredged from the Thames. It's one of the latest models, only just developed. But it's been in the water for over a thousand years. And when the android is reactivated, it has a message – a warning that can only be delivered to a man named the Doctor.

The Doctor and his friends must solve a mystery that has spanned over a thousand years. Travelling backwards and forwards in time, they must unravel the threads of an ancient plot. If they fail, the deadly alien Squall will devour the world…

A thrilling, all-new adventure featuring the Doctor, Amy and Rory, as played by Matt Smith, Karen Gillan and Arthur Darvill in the spectacular hit series from BBC Television.

Coming soon from BBC Books:

DOCTOR ⬛ WHO
Borrowed Time

by Naomi Alderman

£6.99 ISBN 978 1 849 90233 5

Andrew Brown never has enough time. No time to call his sister, no time to prepare for that important presentation at the bank where he works… The train's late, the lift jams, the all-important meeting's started by the time he arrives. Disaster.

If only he'd had just a little more time.

Time is the business of Mr Symington and Mr Blenkinsop. They'll lend Andrew Brown some time – at a very reasonable rate of interest. If he was in trouble before he borrowed time, things have just got a lot worse.

Detecting a problem, the Doctor, Amy and Rory go undercover at the bank. The Doctor's a respected expert, and Amy's his trusted advisor. Rory has a job in the post room. But they have to move fast to stop Symington and Blenkinsop before they cash in their investments. The Harvest is approaching.

A thrilling, all-new adventure featuring the Doctor, Amy and Rory, as played by Matt Smith, Karen Gillan and Arthur Darvill in the spectacular hit series from BBC Television.